Murder with Bengali Characteristics

Also by Shovon Chowdhury

The Competent Authority (2013)

Murder with Bengali Characteristics

a novel

Shovon Chowdhury

ALEPH

ALEPH

ALEPH BOOK COMPANY
An independent publishing firm
promoted by *Rupa Publications India*

Published in India in 2015 by
Aleph Book Company
7/16 Ansari Road, Daryaganj
New Delhi 110002

Copyright © Shovon Chowdhury 2015

The author has asserted his moral rights.

All rights reserved.

This is a work of fiction. Names, characters, places and incidents are either the product of the author's imagination or are used fictitiously and any resemblance to any actual persons, living or dead, events or locales is entirely coincidental.

No part of this publication may be reproduced, transmitted, or stored in a retrieval system, in any form or by any means, without permission in writing from Aleph Book Company.

ISBN: 978-93-82277-79-8

1 3 5 7 9 10 8 6 4 2

Printed and bound in India by Replika Press Pvt. Ltd.

This book is sold subject to the condition that it shall not, by way of trade or otherwise, be lent, resold, hired out, or otherwise circulated without the publisher's prior consent in any form of binding or cover other than that in which it is published.

*This one's for my mum.
She's from Bhobanipur.*

DISCLAIMER

Legal experts have certified that this work of art (henceforth referred to as 'art') does not, in any way, hurt sentiments, outrage the modesty of women, contravene the articles of the Indian Telegraph Act of 1885, or undermine the unity, integrity and stability of the Republic of India. This certification is for legal purposes only, and should not be construed to certify the quality of humour contained herein, or hereunder, as the case may be.

'Lies written in ink cannot disguise truth written in blood.'
–Lu Xun

1

'You were the last person to talk to him while he was alive, sir.'

The old party member lay on the bed, frozen in the act of choking. *The Complete Works of Sharat Chandra Chatterjee, Volume 7*, lay on his chest. His spectacles were broken, his hands were twisted. Death had come suddenly. His thumbs were missing.

Inspector An Li frowned. He was standing in a small hut in the village of Motipur, near Jhargram, in the heart of Maoist country. Which ought to be all one country, now that China was in charge of Bengal, but the Maoists were waiting for the situation to stabilize. It was officially known as the Liberated Zone of Junglemahal. It was slightly larger than Belgium.

He looked down at the shrunken, lifeless body, a hint of sadness in his clear, calm eyes. 'That's all I want,' Gao Yu had once said. 'A man with kind eyes and nice shoulders, who can make me laugh once in a while, and punch out people when I ask him to.' She had often tried to make him do more with his hair, but he preferred it cropped close to the skull. It saved time in the morning.

On the face of it, it was an open-and-shut case. It had thug written all over it, right down to the silver coin next to the pillow. Inspector Li was skeptical about the thug menace. The only shadow creatures he knew worked for the Ministry of Internal

Security. Besides, he preferred facts to assumptions. Facts were solid. Assumptions had a way of changing. For example, he had assumed that his wife would stay with him, but the fact was she was shacking up with a businessman in Beijing who had a life-size replica of the White House in his garden. She had become the businessman's top squeeze, and was bound to displace his wife in due course. Gao Yu and he used to be the Romeo and Juliet of the Beijing police, the tough cop and the hooker with the heart of gold. Li had always known she might leave him, but did it have to be for someone with leopard-print underwear and a diamond-studded cell phone? It was why he had asked for a Calcutta posting, after twenty years in Beijing. He couldn't stand all the sympathy.

The victim was a senior clerk in the fisheries department, and a lifelong party member. He was trotted out of the closet during elections, and trotted back in afterwards. He was one of the Men in Dhotis. The party needed a thin layer of clean white dhotis, a garment representative of old-school communists, for all the goons to hide behind. It also represented a rejection of Western influences, such as trousers. Several neighbours had expressed their regrets, and they seemed to be sincere. The dead man used to spend his evenings teaching local children for free. He would give a couple of biscuits, which was all he could afford, to the poor ones.

Inspector Li picked up the dead man's wallet. It was threadbare and patchy, like a dog with skin disease. It was also evidence. He took out the few tattered notes inside. He would give them to one of the neighbours for the funeral, and add a little bit more, for luck. The rest of its contents, he would study at leisure. He tucked in a visiting card, which seemed to be in Japanese. He felt a brief spasm of revulsion. He had been trained to hate the Japanese. The political climate had changed recently, so he was training himself to stop. China ruled Asia now. They were all one big happy family. The Japanese were the sons, the Koreans were the brothers, and the Bengalis were the idiot cousins. They hadn't had time to figure out where people from places like Nagaland and Mizoram fit. They were too busy chasing them around the jungle. They were remarkably difficult to catch, and unexpectedly warlike. Casualties were heavy, and rising. The whole thing was far less fraternal than had originally been envisaged. Inspector Li was fond of travel, but that was one area he didn't want to see in a hurry. In hindsight, joining North Tibet and South Tibet hadn't been such a good idea either, creating one vast province where everyone hated them. Between the Indians and them, there were more soldiers in the Indian subcontinent than anywhere else on the planet. The Assam Occupation Force alone was bigger than the entire US Army. Life was no picnic. For most Chinese officers in the New Territories, Calcutta was like a rest cure.

A single gunshot rang out, somewhere in the distance. A CPM goon squad, probably. Or a Maoist execution. Or the People's Armed Police, although they tended to be more liberal with ammunition. Or maybe it was barbarian-on-barbarian violence. It was none of his business. He had a crime of his own to investigate.

Inspector Li picked up the dead man's mobile. It was surprisingly advanced for such a poor man—a limited edition Heavenly Body i26. The last call was to Bijli Bose. Could it really be him? The patriarch of the Communist Party of India (Marxist)? The grand old man of the party? He was reputed to be 121 years old. He had kept himself young by sucking the blood of the youth of Bengal, according to one version. Others thought it was because he drank nothing but the finest Scotch. Could this poor old man have been in touch with such an exalted personage? Perhaps they were old party comrades, just spending an evening chatting about their days of struggle. It seemed unlikely. From what he had heard, Bijli Bose was not sentimental.

This was the point where he was supposed to forget he had seen his name. No one messed around with former politburo members, even if they were darkies. It was a matter of principle. And this one was special. This one was held in high esteem by the Motherland. He had helped prepare the way. Nothing good could come from pursuing this.

He took out his own phone, noted the number, and called. 'Hello?' said a dry, quavering voice, echoing faintly, like a voice from the crypt. The video took time to kick in. 'Hello,' said the voice again, and then Bijli Bose shimmered into view. He was the Living Mummy. There was no flesh on his face, just paper dry skin stretched tight across bone, thin wisps of hair across an egg-like head.

'Who?' he whispered.

Bijli Bose spoke very little, to conserve energy, except when he was having fun, or when money was involved. Despite assurances from the Resurrection Engineers, he feared that his new lifespan was limited.

Inspector Li waved briefly. He refused to salute a mobile phone.

'I have a party member of yours…'

'Who is dead. Yes.'

'News travels fast.'

A smile flitted across his thin slit mouth.

'You were the last person alive to talk to him, sir.'

Bijli Bose remained still for a while. Had he fallen asleep? His eyes were still open. Inspector Li waited patiently.

'Come. Tomorrow. Morning,' said Bijli Bose.

He remained on screen, mouth slightly agape, until a servant stepped into the frame and disconnected.

Inspector Li put the phone down and had one last look at the victim. A woman, weeping silently, was trying to put his limbs in order. Someone else came in with flowers. They covered his body with a crumpled, fraying sheet.

2

'Why do you think they still have mounted police in Calcutta?'

'I'll stick it in your father's ear!' roared the young man, supporting his wounded colleague, who was struggling to pick up a stone near his feet.

'Oye! Oye! Oye!' said a voice from the crowd across the street. It was a mob of wiry young men, with a soft centre, consisting of several plump men and a middle-aged lady in spectacles. The middle-aged lady was screaming dementedly, waving her fists in the air, but her voice was too thin to carry. They were losing the verbals, and she knew it. The other side were far more robust and poetic. It was time to escalate. Three of the boys broke free and charged. Their shirts were open and their pants were tight. One of them carried a placard which said 'Not forgetting, never forget!' The others held their ranks and hurled missiles. Their aim was terrible. 'Call your father,' screamed one of them, 'I want to play ping pong with his balls!'

A battered police jeep was parked on the corner of Chowringhee and Park Street. The policemen were sharing a cigarette. This kind of thing happened all the time. It would have been rude to interrupt. People valued good manners above all else, here in Calcutta, capital of the Bengal Protectorate.

The march of tradition was halted by foreign elements. Two sleek, black personnel carriers drove up, and parked themselves in the middle of the road. Genuine Chinese policemen from the Ministry of Internal Security leaped nimbly from their vehicles and fanned out. They were not to be confused with the People's Armed Police, who spent most of their time spying on the Ministry of Internal Security, and made sure everyone met their execution quotas. They reported to a completely different faction of the Standing Committee, although no one was quite sure which one.

The Calcutta Police dropped their cigarettes, got back in their jeep, and drove away. The Chinese were supposed to be advisors, but everyone knew the score. The Internal Security troops carefully and deliberately shot a few of the hooligans on the edge of the melee. Then they waded in and methodically beat the crap out of the rest. They remained expressionless throughout. Their movements were precise. They spoke very little. As usual, they took all the fun out of it. With the local police, on the rare occasions that they took action, there was blood and passion, the hurling of mighty curses, mothers and sisters invoked in vain, blows exchanged in anger. The lunge. The clutch. The heave into the van. There was a certain intimacy. With the Chinese, the whole process was soulless. It was like batting against a bowling machine. The miscreants were soon trooping into custody, heads bowed, dispirited. The language barrier made things worse. What was the point in asking a man to fry an omelette on his mother's cunt if he couldn't understand what you were saying?

As a result of what would later be filed by Crazy Wu as Chowringhee Mass Incident No. 39, Verma and Agarwal were late. They had been hurrying towards Park Street, where all the bars were. Many people had found themselves similarly delayed. A few of the thirstier ones had tried to mingle with the rioters and slip through, and were now en route to the lock-up, unable to explain that it was alcohol and not disloyalty that had motivated their actions. Now that the rioters had been dispersed, eager patrons were jostling each other, stopping occasionally to gape at the pornographic magazines for sale on the crumbling footpath, their paper-screen covers shimmering in the evening light.

Soon, Verma and Agarwal were standing in front of Olypub. They took a moment to look up fondly at the sign, which was still crooked. The doorman was inside, in the corridor, slumped in a chair. He was in his seventies, too young to be a waiter. It was a sore point with him. He ignored them as they entered. No one had tipped him in decades. He was nursing his resentment well, and biding his time. They climbed the rickety stairs. The stench was like a fog. The air was full of smoke, and intellectual banter.

They could just as well have met in Agarwal's enormous family complex on Lord Sinha Road, built to resemble an ocean liner, where alcohol was taboo, and everyone secretly drank in their rooms, but they had fond memories of Park Street. They were drinking buddies from college, when their funds had been low. They sat at their usual table. The waiter brought them chilli chicken and whisky. The chilli chicken was terrible, the whisky harsh and raw. The helpings of both were lavish. This was why Agarwal swore by the place. He was an active seeker of value. His fortunes had been built on this skill. Rats scurried under the tables, stopping occasionally to sniff their feet. Verma was relieved that they were ordinary rats, not the semi-sentient goblin creatures of the Dead Circle in New New Delhi. Calcutta had never been nuked, and had kept it that way by inviting in the Chinese. It was ten years since the war. The Indians had rebuilt New New Delhi, but the area where Mumbai used to be was still radioactive.

Sanjeev Verma took a sip of his whisky. It burnt his throat. He was going soft thanks to all the Blue Label. His bootlegger provided a regular supply, at prices lower than Scotland. He took another sip. He had to get used to it. If he wanted to maintain a regular supply of Blue Label, he needed Agarwal's help, and Agarwal would faint if he suggested drinking it. He was a cheapskate. He had built a nightclub in his basement so that his children could avoid cover charges. Verma needed his help because the mine in Chhattisgarh which they jointly owned was in extreme jeopardy. It was true that his South African mercenaries were doing an excellent job of beating off the Maoists, despite the fact that they drank their body weight in beer. Luckily, the Maoists in the heartland were heavily invested in the encirclement of Patna, where the fighting was hard. They had no time for petty mining barons like them. But now the clouds of war were looming over his dark house, with the Competent Authority in New New Delhi spoiling for a fight, and the Chinese responding to his insults with equivalent skill and ferocity. If these two titans clashed, their mine would become a war zone, and their business would go straight to hell. It would almost certainly be confiscated by the Ministry of Defence, which had diversified over the years. His cousin Mehta had proved unhelpful in the matter of hiring the Indian Army, which would have established the sort of patron-client relationship that was invaluable in a situation like this. It was time to look beyond family. His father had always emphasized the value of family, but Verma had never been convinced. His generation trusted friends more. He had flown down to Calcutta, getting shot down only once in the process, in the hope that Agarwal would be able to do something. He had patron-client relationships of his own. So far, he had spent just a few hours in the city, but he was beginning to have his doubts.

'This type of thing happens all the time here?' he asked. 'What about Chinese discipline?'

'Bengalis are not so easy to discipline,' said Agarwal, who was Marwari. 'Believe me, we've being trying for generations.' He spoke fluent Bengali himself. His family had spent over a hundred years in Calcutta, watching it transform from British to Communist to Chinese, with little bouts of anarchy in between. According to legend, the family had emigrated from Rajasthan with just a blanket and a small water jug, although it was hard to imagine all of them fitting under one blanket. It had been a large family, even then. Their women were notoriously fertile. They had been at the forefront of the Marwari takeover of the Bengal economy, driven by a combination of the Marwari talent for making money, and the Bengali conviction that such things were beneath them.

'The band of our business is getting bajao-ed, boss!' said Verma. His voice was booming, befitting his size. Several of the other patrons looked up disapprovingly, interrupted in their discussions of fiction and poetry. They were bhadralok, proper people, not like the lumpen on the street. Those were the little people. Little people had loud voices, due to their lack of refinement. 'Our case is closing. Our asses are being taken. Our ganesh is flipping. As it is, we have to worry about the Maoists. Once they take Patna, they'll turn their full attention to us. Then our story is finished.'

'Maoists your side are still very violent,' said Agarwal, 'the ones this side are much more peaceful. They have allied with the Chinese to create a better society.'

'Forget about society,' said Verma. 'What did society ever do for us? If a war starts now, we're jacked out of shape. I was hoping we could start some sort of gadar here, so that the Chinese get nervous. Then they'll be too busy suppressing the Bongs to think about war. But it looks like there's already gadar here. Then why are the Chinese taking pangas? Are they mad or what?'

Agarwal tittered. 'What, that little thing you just saw? You should see what happens after a Mohun Bagan–East Bengal match. Why do you think they still have mounted police in Calcutta?'

Verma gulped down the rest of his whisky and waved at the waiter. This was going to be even tougher than he had thought. New

New Delhi was no picnic, what with all the mutants and the biker boys and Delhi Police, but Calcutta was at a different level. It was surprising. Bongs were so thin, and the ones in New Chittaranjan Park seemed so peaceful. He remembered what a former pickpocket from Calcutta had once told him. 'These Bengalis, they look very thin,' he had said, 'but when they hit you, they hit very hard.' He had clearly been reminiscing.

'So that means that this type of chhota-mota disturbance won't serve any purpose,' said Verma. 'We need a full-on revolution before the Chinese will notice anything.'

An ancient waiter tottered up to their table with a bottle of cheap whisky and a peg measure. Verma estimated his age to be ninety-seven. The unions were strong here. The waiter held up the bottle, like a magician about to do a trick, enabling them to verify its genuineness. He held the peg measure over Verma's glass and poured till it overflowed, partly because it was restaurant policy and partly because his hands shook a lot.

'The Chinese are quite used to it,' said Agarwal. 'In China too, people are restless. But, yes, if there was a full uprising, which fool would try to go to war at the same time? That way, Bengal has already had many revolutions. As you can see, they quickly get agitated. Just not recently.'

'How do we start one?' asked Verma, who was simple and direct in his methods.

This was not the first time that the subject of revolution had been discussed at Olypub, nor would it be the last.

Agarwal knew him well. He was very impatient. He humoured him. They also made serious money from the mine, so he was not totally averse to extreme measures.

'We would need a figurehead. Someone to lead the people. Bengal has had many. Former cricket captain Sourav Ganguly would be a good choice, but he is very aloof. He is not taking an interest. Pishi would also be very good. She was once a tall leader of Bengal, although size-wise she is very small. She is a fighter. She is not scared of anyone, except Maoists. All the local good boys are her devotees. Wherever she leads, they will follow her. If you require gadar, whatever the opposition, there is no better candidate than her. Unfortunately she is currently in a mental institution. The Chinese put political enemies in mental institutions, because obviously anyone who opposes the Party must be insane. Of course, if you are looking for a charismatic figure who can lead the people, why look further than Bijli-uncle? He ruled for nearly thirty years, back in the twentieth century. He was an icon. There is a statue of him in Beijing. Without him, none of this would have been possible.'

'How is he still alive?'

'He was regenerated from some DNA found on a whisky glass. Unfortunately, he regenerated at the same age and condition as when he passed away. Scientists have been puzzled. Still, he is a good choice. But why revolution? Even in Calcutta, revolutions are not so easy to arrange. First let us try to do some fixing.'

Verma perked up. He was from Delhi. He knew all about fixing. 'What type of fixing?' he asked.

'See, Governor Wen, he too is like an uncle to me. Let us first go and meet him. Perhaps he can be helpful.'

'He's the guy in charge here?'

'No one knows who's really in charge here. Different people have different powers. That's their system. But he reports directly to the Young Prince. If he portrays a certain picture, he can influence his thinking. Luckily for us, the Governor is currently in a depressed frame of mind.'

'And why is that?'

'His experience in Bengal has not been good. His condition is said to be fragile. He sings in the garden a lot. This was a punishment posting for him. He used to be Mayor of Chengdu, but simultaneously he got into two-two ghaplas involving shopping malls and sexual disturbances. Or so I hear. Any one thing he could have managed, but the combination was too much for him. He was posted to the Bengal Protectorate. His reproduction permit has also been revoked.'

'Sounds like a real loser.'

'Yes, but his report will still carry weight. I can influence him.'

'In your dreams, or genuinely? This is no time to be fucking around.'

Agarwal had delusions of grandeur, socially. He paid to get his picture taken with film stars. Sometimes they cut his birthday cake. He had not yet slept with a heroine, but he remained optimistic.

'No, no, I know him, bhai. I got him his box at the Royal Calcutta Turf Club. He was supposed to get one anyway, but I pretended that I arranged it. His concubines love it, they dress up and carry pretty umbrellas and go to the races. He is very grateful to me.'

'Well do something quickly, man,' said Verma. 'That fucker back home is unzipping as we speak.'

'He's a big person. We can't just walk in. I know his man, Ganguly. He's actually my man. He's eaten enough from me. He'll fix us up. All it requires is some fixing.'

Verma brightened considerably. It was something to look forward to. He had never fixed a Governor before. He was sure that the methods of doing so would be very different here, with many unexpected nuances and cultural peculiarities. It was true what Sunita said. Travel really did broaden the mind.

3

'He's probably in the bathroom, singing.'

Inspector Li was debriefing Big Chen while soothing music played over the PA system, creating an atmosphere of tranquility. A pretty girl was massaging his shoulders. Conditions had improved considerably at Lal Bazaar, the traditional centre of law enforcement in Bengal, now home to the Calcutta office of the Public Security Bureau. It was like Scotland Yard with lathis, and a greater tolerance for paunches. The comfort and well-being of the security forces was a top priority. Everyone had Wi-Fi enabled swivel chairs, and fluffy monogrammed towels in the bathroom, although the aim of local constables continued to be poor, regardless of what they were shooting with.

Big Chen was immune to such fripperies. He was a tall man with a bullet head and the rough skin of a peasant. He came from a part of China where the towns had names like Kill the Foreigners, Pacify the Hu, Overawe the Barbarians, and Fuck the Eighth Uncle of all Invaders. People often thought he was stupid, and he never contradicted them.

'Find out more about the other victims,' said Li. 'The thugs have been doing this for a while.' He waved the girl away. She was distracting, and besides, they were all snitches. She slid off his table and left the room.

'There were four of them,' said Big Chen. 'All of them were Chinese.'

'Good man,' said Li. 'That means Barin Mondol was their first local victim. Unless they've been killing locals on the side. Might have been filed under local disputes. Find out more about the Chinese victims too. The thugs are supposed to be terrorists. Why did they kill them, and not you or me? I think we need to know.'

Big Chen made a note in his notebook. He preferred using pencils. It was one of the reasons why Li liked him. 'The victim was a teacher,' said Big Chen, 'did you meet any of his students?'

'I couldn't find any,' said Li. 'The locals didn't seem to know. They were poor kids. No one notices poor kids. The principal of the local school might have an idea. You should go meet him. Take Phoni-babu with you. Don't let him beat up anyone.'

'Right,' said Big Chen. Phoni-babu was their local liaison, a hard-bitten veteran with a foul disposition and a deep aversion to work. Some contact with the locals was unavoidable, but Big Chen hated being in Phoni-babu's company. His personal hygiene was deplorable.

'We need to find out more about this New Thug Society, and the local Maoists,' said Li. 'We need to understand the politics of this case. It's always about politics here. It's because they don't have anything else. Sexy Chen would know. He thinks he's a player. Where is he?'

'I can't find him,' said Big Chen, 'He's probably in the bathroom, singing.' Sexy Chen liked the deep resonance that bathroom walls provided him.

'Get him to throw.'

Big Chen whispered into his phone. 'The boss wants you. Throw yourself in, loser,' he said. Relations between the two sergeants were not good. Sexy Chen was a typical Shanghai thruster, all knees and elbows.

Sexy Chen materialized in the centre of the room, shimmering. He was life-sized but slightly transparent, and looking good, as usual. He was adjusting his hair, but he stopped when he saw Li. He had high cheekbones and narrow eyes. His hair was luxuriant. Sexy Chen fantasized about being a pop singer, which was his back-up plan in case he failed to make it to the Central Committee. He was the son of a minor princeling who had shamed his family by running someone over with a BMW and allowing it to get on the news. He had come to the Bengal Protectorate to rebuild his career. He had joined the police because the army was too crowded, and had vowed that he would go back to mainland China only after he had made a name for himself. This meant that he was probably here for life. Meanwhile he was constantly checking all the angles, finding out the right connections, assessing who was up and who was down. Li was down, and couldn't care less. This made him formidable. Sexy Chen issued a sketchy salute.

'What's up, boss?'

'We're investigating a former member of the Politburo,' said Li.

'What?' said Sexy Chen. He went semi-transparent with fear, flickered in and out, and disappeared. Moments later, he burst into the room, in person. He must have been somewhere nearby.

'Don't do it, boss!' he said. 'It's suicide! Remember what the principal at the Beijing Police Academy said. Solve the case gloriously, but be careful where big people are involved.' Sexy Chen planned to betray Inspector Li at some point in order to further his career. He seemed like the disloyal type, and if there was one thing Sexy Chen could not stand, it was disloyalty. But not just yet. The timing had to be right, and he had no desire to go down with him.

'A man is dead,' said Li. 'He was a decent man, I think. You're going to help us find out who killed him.'

'Who's the Politburo member?' asked Sexy Chen, sticking to the point.

'I should have said *former* Politburo member. His name is Bijli Bose. He ran Bengal for years, before the war, before they invited us in. He's been a loyal supporter of the Motherland. It's just that for a long time no one knew which Motherland.'

'A darkie?' Sexy Chen relaxed slightly. That made things easier, but he would remain vigilant.

'I talked to him briefly. Seemed like a tough nut,' said Li. 'Find out more about him. Now tell me about the Maoists. There's a local camp nearby. What have they been up to lately?'

Sexy Chen relaxed further. The boss wanted to gossip. His loyalty was suspect, but he had his good points. He was quite human with his subordinates.

'The liberated zone closest to the Protectorate is Junglemahal. They've been ruling it for years now. The boys over there are supremely chilled. They're focusing more on theatre and floriculture. Discipline has been going to hell. Some of them have come back from the Patna front. Others are local recruits who just want to stay home. They're not as interested in revolution as they used to be. Violence is way down. They haven't executed too many class enemies lately, although this could be because there are none left.'

Would Barin Mondol classify as a class enemy, Li wondered. Technically, he worked for the government, but in a low-level clerical position in the Fisheries Department. He would have to go there. He would also have to visit some of these supremely chilled Maoists. They were very different from the Maoists back home, who were busy identifying revisionists and waiting for popular sentiment and circumstances to align. Meanwhile, they were raising funds by selling Mao memorabilia.

'Big Chen is finding out about the other victims. You find

out more about the thugs. They're a secret society. Go check with Crazy Wu. He's good with secrets.'

'Please, boss, not Crazy Wu,' begged Sexy Chen. 'His skin is covered in creepy-crawlies. The last time I met him, he and his duplicate spent most of their time cracking jokes about me.'

Crazy Wu was their Information Officer. He never came out of the basement. His primary job was to prevent the public from getting too much information. He helped suppress reports, comments, paintings, photographs, memes, graphic novels, music, films, books, art installations, theatre, interpretative dance performances, mime and any other form of self-expression which contained the wrong type of thinking. He was a member of the Happy Cow Army, a hacker collective, which had once roamed proud and free. Now they were government employees. They created software that hunted disloyalty across networks and devices, ensuring that even the original files were destroyed. Nowadays, when a book was banned, it disappeared forever. Because Crazy Wu spent so much time making knowledge disappear, no one knew more than him. Li had figured this out long ago. Crazy Wu was unpredictable, but for some reason he approved of Li.

Inspector Li looked down at his phone. It was Gao Yu. In the old days, he had often ignored her calls, because he was busy. Now that it was too late, he never made that mistake. 'Just go,' he said, as he dismissed Sexy Chen. Gao Yu appeared on his screen. It had to be a screen. There was no way he could afford long-distance holo. Her eyes were just as alive as he remembered. She seemed to have grown fairer, but her nose was still crooked. Her pimp had punched her in the face. She had knifed him in the groin. Her police record had made her out to be a one-woman crime spree. He remembered well. That was the second time they had brought her in.

'What did you do with my red shoes?' she demanded. He

braced himself. He knew that expression. It meant trouble.

Li tried hard to remember. 'I sent everything back in a box,' he said. 'You didn't have much.'

'You know how hard I worked to save money for those shoes from what you gave me every month?'

Li remembered. She had been a good wife, for a while.

'I didn't think you would need them,' he said gently. 'Your new man could buy you a whole shoe factory, if he wanted. You could have an Italian cobbler living in your dressing room. Why would you need old shoes?'

Gao Yu was waving something. It looked like a weapon. 'Look at this! Look! You couldn't keep them properly? Was it so much trouble? The heel is broken. I used to love these shoes.' She was working herself up. He could see it. He did what he always did.

'Send me a picture,' he said. 'I'll save up and buy you new ones. I have to rush, pretty. I have to go back to a village near the jungle, and then I have to meet a politician. He could be involved in a murder.'

Gao Yu hung up on him.

4

'He doesn't know ABCD,
but his house is like the Taj Mahal.'

It was a village of thatched roofs and naked children. Nothing much had changed in hundreds of years. Li's car was the most modern object within a fifty-mile radius. Village boys had gathered round it, peering inside, running their hands all over, whispering to each other. The car put up with it for a while, before letting off a blast on its siren. The boys scattered. The car called after them. 'Juveniles! Remember to study the Six New Thought Processes! And always wash your hands before meals!'

The old lady sat on her porch, a stainless steel plate on her lap, picking stones out of a pile of rice. She threw them at her goat who ignored them. She bared her toothless gums at Li. 'All these teeth were taken from me by ration shop rice,' she said. 'However much you try, you can never get them all.'

'It's the same everywhere,' said Li.

'Barin-babu never mixed with us much,' she said, 'even though we lived next door. He did come to my husband's funeral, though. He ate very little.'

'Too high class?' asked Li.

'What class will a Mondol have? Nothing like that. In the morning he would do his puja, bathe-shathe, go off to office. He was a small-time gorment babu. Not even smart enough to make money. Came back in the evening, read his books, ate dinner, slept. He was always reading books. Very big scholar he was. One of my nephews was like that, always reading. Bhodai, go and have your bath, I would say. Just coming, he would say, two more pages. He never amounted to much. Neither did Barin-babu. What was the point of so much reading? Barin-babu lived in a raw hut, just like me. These are all useless pursuits. Look at Geju. He doesn't know ABCD, but his house is like the Taj Mahal. He has his own cinema hall, and his maid is automatic. Spoilt girls come for parties to his house.'

'What about his students? Do you remember any of them?'

'I think one of them was Fatima's husband-sister's son, but I'm not sure. Five-six of them there were, age would be twelve-thirteen. He was chewing their heads, I can tell you. What's the point in teaching village boys? What good can come of it? Will they become magistrates? And even if they do, what comes or goes for us? Moyna's auntie-mother-in-law in Narayanpur, she became a magistrate. Now her son lives in America. People say he has a helicopter. What good did it do the village?'

Li noticed his car hovering near Barin Mondol's hut. It was in stealth mode. It had retractable tentacles, with which it could apprehend suspects, provided they weren't too agile. It must have spotted something suspicious. Li let it be. It could well be a cow. Its ability to distinguish between humans and animals was limited.

'So you've known him for many years,' he said.

'All my life. He was a few years older than me. His father was a railway guard. Used to beat his wife. Barin spent his whole life in the village. Only his college he did in Calcutta. He came back very modern. I thought he would marry a modern girl, but he never married. He was a communist. I don't know what else he learnt in college, but communism he learnt very well. Everything was party, party, party with him. Party was his father, Party was his mother, Party was his children. All of us will be free, he would tell me, just you wait. In those days he was very active. In the beginning, Party did some good things. But after that, it became all goondas, like that Geju.'

'I thought you liked Geju,' said Li.

'Who else is there to like? He's the only person. Whatever has to be done, he has to do. We had thought the Party ruling means everyone in the village will prosper, but actually they had a quota. It was one person per village, approved by the Party. Mostly they are the goonda-badmaash type. Whatever kind of number-two business in the locality, that person will do. Seeing all this, Barin became depressed. Only during election time, Geju and the other boys would come, saying, come, come, Barin-da, you are well respected, come and ask for votes. The Party requires your service. Barin would go. After elections, they forgot about him, until next time. This was their system. In this way, the Party ruled. In Bengal, we prefer polite people. Seeing polite people in front, people were reassured. After some years, the goondas decided, now the public knows us well, there is no need to hide. Naturally by then we knew them, because they were taking money from all of us. From that time onwards, they fought elections on their own. Polite people became unimportant. The Party never called Barin again.'

He sounded a little like an old-school Maoist, thought Li, as opposed to the neo-Maoists, who had websites. You could still see them in Beijing parks on Sundays, waving flags and singing from the Little Red Book. Gao Yu used to point at them and laugh. 'Losers! As if anyone's going to follow people dressed like that! China needs fashion, baby!'

'Did he still have links with the Party?'

'Who knows?' said the old lady. 'We hardly talked towards the end. But one thing I will say, he was a decent man, a polite person. Not like all those small people. Nowadays, wherever you look, the country is covered in small people.' She turned her head and spat on the ground.

'What was he doing with the boys?'

'He always worked for the country. It's just that as he got older, the work became smaller. Towards the end, he thought about education a lot. In the evening, he would teach some poor boys. English-finglish he was teaching them. Of course, nowadays you can put the language straight in the brain, with some type of injection, I've heard. Just the way you must have learnt Bengali. But you still have to practice. Your Bengali is quite sweet, for a chinkie.'

Li ducked his head to acknowledge the compliment. He tried speaking it whenever he could. Most of his colleagues never bothered, so when they did, they sounded like circus freaks. Reading was even harder. No software was able to translate *Ananda Bazar Patrika*, a popular local newspaper, in which the language was high-flown and literary, and the descriptions of meals very detailed.

An alarm went off in his hat. He whipped it off and clutched his head. He wished he could control the volume. It was the car. It had hovered back into view, clutching a little boy in its tentacles. The boy was struggling silently, arms and legs waving in the air. He had a narrow, angry face, streaked with tears. 'Suspect apprehended!' said the car. 'Suspect apprehended!'

'Excuse me, mother,' said Li, and walked over to his vehicle, which was waiting patiently, the struggling boy firmly in its grip. 'Where did you find him?' he asked.

'Suspect was trying to enter scene of the crime,' said the car. 'Appears to be a human juvenile. Suspect is unarmed. His pockets contain sixty-two rupees and an A-card. Should I interrogate suspect? Please, Inspector Li? No one ever lets me interrogate suspects. I practise a lot when you park me.'

Inspector Li put the car on mute. 'Let the boy go,' he said. The tentacles relaxed. The suspect collapsed to the ground. He stood up and wiped his eyes angrily with the back of his hand. He looked about twelve, but it was hard to be sure. Most boys here were small for their age. It was basic nutrition. With every generation, the Chinese were becoming bigger and the Indians smaller.

'You were his student, weren't you?' said Li.

The boy nodded silently. He was used to keeping secrets. Li smiled at him. 'Would you like to come for a ride in my car?' he asked.

'Can we fly?' asked the boy, his face lighting up. 'I've never been in the sky.'

It was tight. He had enough fuel to fly for six minutes. Fuel had been in short supply ever since the Saudis had run out in '33. Nowadays, they spent most of their time with their camels.

'Why not?' said Li.

'Can you stop him from talking, though?' asked the boy. 'He talks too much, and he's stupid. I hate it when stupid people talk too much.'

'I'll shut him off if it gets too bad,' said Li, 'but he's got a right to talk if he wants to, doesn't he?'

The boy looked at the car thoughtfully. He remembered his teacher.

'I suppose he does,' he said.

5

'I have no objection to you shaving your brother-in-law. It seems perfectly harmless to me...'

'Sir, this is for you, sir,' said Agarwal, placing the sandalwood Ganesha before him. It would look quite nice on top of the small teakwood bookcase just behind the Governor. There was a small Chinese flag on his table, next to the black-and-red flag of the Bengal Protectorate—a silhouette of the Poet Rabindranath with his hand on the head of a tiger. It was the only flag in the world featuring a beard. On the rich wood-panelled wall behind the table hung portraits of Chairman Mao and Mahatma Gandhi. They were looking in different directions.

Governor Wen raised the idol to his nose and sniffed it. This was an unexpected result of their religious policy. The anti-proselytization laws had been withdrawn to increase religious conflict amongst the locals, even though they were managing perfectly well on their own. Conversion work had started immediately amongst the immigrant Chinese, who were presumed to be godless. This worried Governor Wen. The immigrants were mostly low-class riff-raff from rural areas, with a sprinkling of urban undesirables, and a selection of senior citizens. They'd been removed to reduce social tension in the mainland. Personally, he didn't care who prayed to what, but he knew the other members of the Central Committee back home would take a very dim view if too many of them were converted into Hindus. China was now a majority Christian nation. Things were bad enough already. Many of the immigrants had started playing carom instead of mah-jongg. They refused to drink Feichang Cola, preferring the harsh buzz of Thums Up. They often demonstrated a disrespectful attitude towards security forces. Some of the most depraved had started eating with their hands. It defeated the whole purpose of colonization. It was easy for the Committee to criticize. They didn't have to deal with the Indians. They had no idea how tricky they were.

Take the two specimens in front of him. One of them was an Indian Indian, from New New Delhi, while the other was their own Indian, from Calcutta. One was a tall, strong, white devil, while the other was a short, fat, black devil. He could never remember which one was from where. Not that it mattered. They were all equally untrustworthy. He never said this to their faces, of course. His management style was avuncular and went well with his girth and his bald pate. He would never make it to the Standing Committee, whose members were trim and interchangeable, with their improbably dark hair and their identical dark suits.

'Such a pretty little thing, isn't it, Wang?' he said.

'It's a foolish toy for ignorant rice buckets,' said Propagandist Wang, sneering. He sneered a lot. He was a thin, angular man with a wispy goatee. He looked like a cross between John Lennon and a praying mantis. He sat in a chair behind the Governor, to one side. He liked viewing things from an angle. While there was some debate on the subject, and both General Zhou and Crazy Wu were strong contenders, most people agreed that he was the most powerful person in the Protectorate. His job was to promote correct thinking.

Agarwal and Verma were sitting across the table. Verma was looking at his tea suspiciously. There were unidentified objects at the bottom of the cup. 'As your loyal subjects, Your Highness, we have come to you with valuable information,' said Agarwal.

Governor Wen disliked information. So far as he was concerned, the less he knew the better. 'Can't you share it with Ganguly?' he asked. Ganguly was his assistant. He was a great source of comfort to him in these times of trouble. 'He's very good with information.'

'Sir, this is for your ears only, sir,' said Agarwal, 'It requires the involvement of the highest levels of the Party.'

'Are you going to tell us, or are you waiting for the next Party Conference in Beijing?' snapped Propagandist Wang.

Agarwal remained unfazed by his rudeness. His father had taught him two things very early in life. Politeness doesn't cost money, he had said, and insults cannot hurt you. Agarwal had lived his life by these principles. So long as they left his wallet alone, he was fine with whatever they said to him. He drew his chair closer.

'We are hearing whispers of war,' he said.

Right on cue, there was the sound of gunfire from just beyond the French window. Moments later, General Zhou stepped through briskly, holding a clipboard.

'Here's another batch for you to sign,' he said, cheerfully, placing the clipboard in front of the Governor.

'Do I really have to?' asked Governor Wen. He hated signing death warrants. All he wanted was some peace and quiet, and a moderate selection of concubines. But General Zhou had quotas to fill, and he was always in a hurry. Members of the elite were executed on the Governor's lawn, out of deference to local sentiment. Poorer people were taken behind the chemical sheds. Things had changed on the mainland, but in the provinces, traditional methods of governance applied.

'You should join us,' said General Zhou. 'The boys will be thrilled.'

'Chairman Mao used to supervise executions personally,' added

Propagandist Wang, primly. Governor Wen signed the order. General Zhou swung round on his heel and left through the French window.

'Sir, you are facing the possibility of war, sir,' said Agarwal, slightly put out. He had expected to make more impact than this. 'We are hearing whispers. Loud whispers.'

The Governor sat bolt upright. His paunch pushed the heavy oak table forward a few inches. 'Who is whispering about war?' he demanded. 'And why can't they speak up?'

'Sir, it's the Competent Authority, sir,' said Agarwal. 'The CA. He's the man who rules India. People think it's the PM, but she's only there for the TV channels. Between you and me, he's taken leave of his senses.'

The stress of sitting upright made the Governor lose focus for a moment. 'I have no objection to you shaving your brother-in-law,' he said, mixing him up with an earlier petitioner. 'It seems perfectly harmless to me, and does not affect the harmoniousness of society in any way. As far as I know, it's not forbidden by the law. Is it Propagandist Wang?' he asked anxiously.

Propagandist Wang bit his lip. Whatever he had to say to this turtle product could not be said in front of barbarians. Agarwal was perplexed. The Governor was degenerating from vegetable to mineral with astonishing rapidity. He would have to ask Ganguly to dilute his medication.

'Sir, it's the truth, sir,' he said. 'He believes the telepath attack was conducted by you. Any minute he may declare war, sir.'

The Indian telepathic corps had recently been attacked. Many of them had been hospitalized. Some had disappeared. Others were drinking in bars. As per instructions of the Competent Authority, India's premier investigative agency, the CBI, had immediately reached the conclusion that the Chinese were responsible. They were scheduled to find supporting evidence within seven days.

'Did we conduct the telepath attack?' Governor Wen asked

Wang, by now thoroughly confused. Propagandist Wang shook his head, not trusting himself to speak. It was true, what people said. Inbreeding was the single biggest problem facing the CCP.

Governor Wen felt personally betrayed. He spent all his time trying to be nice to everyone, but what good did it ever do? 'What should we do?' he asked, wishing someone would tell him. 'Should we leave? What about all the immigrants?'

'New Bengalis!' barked Propagandist Wang.

'Yes, yes, let's quibble over semantics,' said Governor Wen, irritated into testiness, 'that's the best way to deal with this. Let's beat each other up with dictionaries while the sky falls on our heads. Do you have any suggestions?' he asked Agarwal hopefully.

'Sir, there is a way, sir,' said Agarwal, 'Something that only a tall leader like you can do.'

This did not sound good. Governor Wen waited apprehensively.

'Bengalis are very excitable, sir. Historically they have caused many disturbances. Traditionally their attitude is poor. Right from Mughal times, there are reports which confirm this. Add to that the current situation. The New Thug Society is strangling people. Maoist behaviour is highly suspect. Telepaths may be reading our brains. File a report with the Party, sir, perhaps exaggerating the situation a little, saying things are very bad, and they should avoid war at all costs. Then you just kowtow to the CA a little, maybe give away a piece of Chhattisgarh, and everything will be peaceful. War will be avoided. You will be like an angel of peace.'

This last bit was a masterstroke. Their mine was in Chhattisgarh. If the Chinese no longer claimed the area, they would stop pushing Maoists in, and Verma and Agarwal would no longer need South African mercenaries. They cost a fortune in vuvuzelas and beer.

'You want me to tell the Standing Committee that the situation in Bengal is going out of control?' asked Governor Wen, unable to believe his ears.

'Only slightly,' said Agarwal, showing a small gap between finger and thumb.

'They'll shoot me!' said Governor Wen.

A single shot rang out in the garden. Governor Wen leaped out of his chair.

General Zhou popped in.

'Sorry, missed one,' he said, and popped out.

'Kowtow,' spat Propagandist Wang. 'No one is going to kowtow. You will write to the Standing Committee immediately demanding more troops, more drones, and more money. We will build up our strength, and boost morale through patriotic songs and audiovisual presentations. We will fly down some Harmony Doctors to re-educate splittists. If anybody from their pathetic little half-country threatens us, we will crush them, once and for all. If they want war, we will give them war.'

'They'll shoot me for that too,' said Governor Wen.

'No, no, sir, never,' said Agarwal, soothingly. 'Not a person of your calibre. It would be too great a loss for the nation. They may confiscate a few companies. Convert one two malls into Jinping Thought Centres. Perhaps freeze one two bank accounts. Nothing more than that, sir.'

'If you think I'm going to report to the Committee that my province is going out of control, you need to have your head examined!'

Agarwal knew when to fold his hand. He drank up his Five Treasures tea. He gave the Governor his business card. He kept changing his address to avoid creditors. 'Sir, please think further,' he said. 'Also, if you need any help writing reports or framing any sort of regulation, kindly let me know.'

He and Verma got up to leave. Verma hung back for a moment, wondering whether to menace them. It was what he usually did. But he deferred to Agarwal's judgement. This was his home ground.

'So what do we do now?" he asked, once they were outside. Agarwal looked remarkably calm for a man whose hopes had just been dashed.

'We'll make an appointment with Ganguly-da, the Governor's assistant,' he said. 'He's very cultured and capable. He's my man. I pay him a small retainer fee. He'll know what to do.'

Verma was not reassured by this.

'I'm sure everyone pays him a small fee,' he said morosely.

6

*'She does it less now because
the hospital is too far away.'*

They were travelling at a height of around forty feet, so they could still recognize people on the ground. 'Hey, look, there's Tuklu!' said the boy, pointing to a slightly depressed young man. He was chivvying a cow out of a half-submerged field of paddy. 'Kareena's got in the rice again! She's a weirdo. She loves water. Hey, Tuklu! Tuklu!'

'He can't hear you,' said Li.

'And look! There's Geju-da's house!'

It was hard to miss. It was the only brick structure in a sea of thatched huts. It had pink walls, orange windows, and a massive dish on the roof. A drone was hovering in the courtyard. As they watched, it delivered a swift electric shock to the man who was sweeping the backyard. He started sweeping faster.

Inspector Li had no time for sightseeing. He was running out of fuel. The back-up battery was only good for surface travel. He rapped his knuckle on the dashboard. 'Find us a nice, quiet place where we can land in the next four minutes,' he said. There was a brief pause, as the car consulted its database.

'Here are some suitable options,' it said. 'The spot where Deputy Secretary Jeng distributed shoes to the poor. The spot where Party

Secretary Zhao unveiled a portrait of the Young Prince. The spot where Commissioner Wang enjoyed the view, and took a photo that was much admired on Weibo. Each one has a memorial stone or plaque, to enable identification of the exact location.'

'Take us to a place where no one from the Party has ever been,' said Li.

'How about the spot where the wife of a Central Committee member gave a musical performance, bringing great joy to the masses?' said the car. 'It's very picturesque, right next to the river. There's a mango orchard nearby. According to local legend, witches may be living in it. The technical term for them is shankhchunnis. They can extend their arms to great lengths, while still sitting in their tree. This helps them to reach through windows and pluck babies out of their cradles.'

'Some other time,' said Li.

The car hovered indecisively for a moment before swooping ahead. A few minutes later it was landing in a football field. There was a small crop of dull grey buildings nearby. The football field was a good choice. Given the performance of the national football team, no official in his right mind would want to be associated with the sport. The Chinese football team was a mystery. It was strange that a country of a billion people was unable to produce eleven men who could challenge Brazil. Despite being bullied and threatened constantly, their performance never seemed to improve.

The car sank its wheels into the grass with a happy sigh. Its doors swung open. A gunshot rang out in the distance. They could see small figures running about in the cluster of buildings across the field. 'We should probably stay in the car,' said Inspector Li.

'Don't worry,' said the boy, hopping out. He sat down in the grass. 'It's just the students' union. It's election time at the engineering college. They use country revolvers. The bullets don't go very far.'

Li settled down next to him. He took a KitKat out of his pocket and handed it to the boy. The boy examined it thoroughly, turning it over and over. He had never held one in his hands before. He ripped it open and nibbled on it cautiously. He nibbled and nibbled, taking his time, until it was finished. He licked the wrapper thoroughly. He read what was written on it, lips moving silently, as if memorizing it. He folded it up carefully and put it in his pocket.

'You miss him, don't you?' said Li.

The boy's face crumpled but he did not cry. 'He was the only person who ever talked to us,' he said. 'He didn't have much money but he gave us biscuits.' He fished out a crumpled wrapper. 'See?'

'I'll get whoever killed him,' said Li. 'But I need your help. His neighbour says he didn't know anyone, but that can't be true. If no one knew him, why would anyone kill him?'

'Everybody knew him,' said the boy. 'It's because you're a policeman. People say it's better to wrestle a tiger than talk to a policeman. They can lock anyone up, and it costs money to get out. None of us have money. Is it true you can lock anyone up?'

'Well the laws here are very strong,' said Li, 'you're ruled by a penal code which was put together in 1861. This was just after you revolted against the British in 1857.'

He could see the boy's lips moving. 1857. 1861. He was memorizing. He caught Li looking at him. 'I like remembering things,' he said by way of explanation.

'The whole point behind those laws,' said Li, 'was that the natives should never raise their heads again. You're still ruled by those laws. You never did raise your heads again, so it must have worked very well. When we first came here from China, everyone was highly impressed. People say we're a police state, but your laws are much worse. There's this sedition law, for example. Anyone can be picked up for showing disaffection to the government. You know what that means?'

'Not feeling affection,' said the boy. 'Like Haridas and his wife. They have disaffection. She beats him up regularly. When he asks why, she says why do I need a reason? When he's drunk he can't stop her, and anyway she's bigger than him. She does it less now because the hospital is too far away.'

'Well if you don't feel affection for the government,' said Li, 'you can be arrested. That's the law. Seeing how well it works here, we recently introduced it in China. So, yes, it's true. We can lock anyone up. But I haven't locked you up, have I? And I took you for a ride in a flying car.'

The boy considered this.

'Geju-da used to know him,' he said. 'Most of us worked for Geju-da.'

'What kind of work do you do?'

'What kind of work would boys like us do?' said the boy. 'We sell things on the streets of Calcutta.'

'What do you sell?'

'This and that,' said the boy evasively. 'Things.'

'Anyone else you can think of?'

'Debu-da used to play chess with him once a week. He's the local head of the Mao-followers. Manik-babu, the chaiwallah, says he's a disgrace to the revolution, and should be shot, but Manik-babu believes everyone should be shot. Debu-da seems like a nice guy. He likes books. He's the reading-writing type.'

'Did your Master look worried about anything?'

'Mister Master was always worried. Whenever we asked him why, he would say he was worried about the country. If you mean was he worried about anything particular, he never told us. But why are you asking so many questions? Wasn't he strangled by thugs?'

'He might have been,' admitted Li. 'Did you see any thugs around the village?'

The boy laughed. 'You're so funny,' he said. 'How will you find out anything if you know nothing? As if anyone can see thugs. They hide in the shadows. They melt in with the rest of us. They're just like you or me. They strike up friendships at tea shops, or give you a lift on their motorcycle. They become your friend. They sit and chat with you, just like we are chatting right now. Then they strangle you, and leave a coin. But you're safe. I don't have a handkerchief. I'm lucky I have pants. That's thanks to Geju-da. It's a matter of prestige for him. "My boys should not look like beggars," he says.'

'So Geju-da takes care of you?'

'Naturally he does. We provide his income. We work on the street, he takes care of permissions.'

'You mean applications and forms?'

'No, I mean money. He pays the police. You also must be getting some. Geju-da says he pays everyone, even the Commissioner.'

'They must have forgotten to give me my share,' said Li. 'Now hand over your A-card.'

The boy hesitated. Once the police had his number, they could locate him through GPS, thanks to the chip embedded in it. It was mandatory to carry the card at all times. When the government had first made A-cards compulsory, they had said it was to provide benefits. But they had never specified who would benefit. Now it was much clearer. Thanks to the A-card, the government could locate anyone any time they wanted. They could also check his bank balance, find out what pizza he had ordered last week, see where he had last gone on holiday, and study any medical procedures he might have undergone recently. Luckily, he was too poor to afford any of these. But the location thing was a problem.

'Someone killed your Mister Master,' said Li, 'I don't know who, and I don't know why. But I do know that if one member of a group is killed, it doesn't always end with him.'

The boy handed over his A-card.

7

*'You can say he is a dreamer,
but he is not the only one.'*

'Oh, that one's in the gap! Rocketing off the bat like a tracer bullet! It's all about timing and placement! What a strike! Terrific blow! That's some outstanding batting by the captain!'

The commentator was standing on a rickety folding chair, with two men on either side in case he fell off in his excitement. The crowd did not go wild immediately. A small group of men around the boundary line clapped furiously. 'Guru! Guru!' they cried. 'What a sot!' They turned and glared at the villagers, who raised a feeble cheer. The villagers were wretchedly poor. Most of them were bare-bodied. A few wore tattered vests. None of them wore pants, just strips of cloth wrapped around their waists. Many people in China still wore ragged pants, but at least they had pants. Big Chen found it hard not to feel contempt for them. Why did none of them want to get ahead? Did they want to stay this way their entire lives? He was equally disgusted by the principal of the local school, whom they had come to see. He was the one in the middle, thrashing the opposition bowlers. Beyond the field, in front of a health centre with no roof, a mixture of rice and dal was being cooked in a huge aluminium drum, over a massive gas stove. A separate table was piled high with choice fillets of bhetki, a type of native fish which was somewhere in the middle of the highly complex local fish hierarchy. Once the match was over, the whole village would celebrate his batting exploits with a feast. What kind of man was he, parading his wealth and influence in front of so many poor people? Wasn't he supposed to be running a school?

'He's a regular Li Gang, is what he is,' muttered Big Chen. 'Thinks he's above the law.'

'You people are so ignorant. It's a good thing I'm here,' said Phoni-babu. 'You don't understand the function of government school employees in Bengal. Their purpose is not education of children. Their purpose is education of the public.' Phoni-babu was a wizened little man of indeterminate age. His hair was wispy but his moustache was pronounced. His A-card said he was twenty-two. His birth certificate had suffered rain damage, so there was no way of verifying this. His approach to policing was traditional. It involved beating up people, taking away their money, and complaining a lot. The Chinese let him make his money and, in return, he helped them out.

He and Big Chen had come to meet the Principal of Motipur Secondary School, hoping that he could help them locate some of Barin-babu's students. In addition to being an educationist, the Principal was a local pillar of the Party. In order to avoid corruption, the Party never paid its workers. It gave them teaching jobs instead.

'The main thing they are teaching is that it is never a good idea to oppose the Party,' explained Phoni-babu. 'They are there in every village. In this way, with the help of school principals and local elder brothers, the Party maintains its grip over Bengal. All this was the brainchild of Pomode-babu, architect of the Party. Bijli Bose was the face of the Party, but Pomode-babu was the man with the bamboo, standing right behind him. He could make strong men wet their pants. Even today, in the middle of the night, mothers tell their restless children, "Little one, go to sleep, otherwise Pomode-babu will come." He used to smoke cigars. His ghost still inhabits their office in Alimuddin Street. Late at night, when the city is still, except for the occasional explosion and cries of the wounded, you can still smell a small amount of cigar smoke in the building. Compared to him, who is this Principal? Pomode-babu used to eat three such people for breakfast.'

A nearby worker overheard them. 'Oye, don't be disrespectful,' he said, 'Our dada is not only a teacher and a pincipaal, he is a leader. He provides vision. A rape case happened here last week. He has come here on behalf of the Party. Investigation is running a little slow. He is showing his solidarity with the villagers by playing a cricket match, after which he will feed everyone. In this way he is demonstrating our commitment to good administration. He is trying to touch the hearts of the people through sporting activities. You can say he is a dreamer, but he is not the only one.'

'This part even I cannot understand,' said Phoni-babu. 'He is making mincemeat out of the local bowling attack. How is this going to cheer them up? It's very likely that none of them will ever play cricket again.'

'What is this game, anyway?' asked Big Chen.

'It's cricket, the game of kings,' said Phoni-babu, 'Look over there. In the ground, behind the Principal, you will see three pieces of wood. You have to defend these pieces of wood from the ball thrown by a person at the other end, with a bigger piece of wood, which you hold in your hand. The umpire keeps an eye on the bowler. If the bowler gets too close to the batsman, he has a better chance of getting him in the testicles. This is frowned upon. In this particular case, the umpire is the Principal's cousin, but it is not compulsory that the batsman and the umpire should be related. As a batsman, you have to get the ball as far away as possible. Also you have to run, and, if possible come back, but before the wicketkeeper gets the ball. He stands right behind you, trying to smash your wood. You have to keep an eye on him. The best wicketkeepers are usually the sneaky type, always trying to get you from the backside. It's their mentality. If you find out that someone is a wicketkeeper, do not trust him. Former captain of India, legendary Sourav Ganguly made this mistake, and as a result his career was hampered.'

'A lofted, terrific shot, straight to the boundary!' cried the commentator. 'This man is on fire! A masterful strike by one of the greatest batsmen Jhargram district has ever seen! What a superb innings this has been!' The Principal raised his bat. It was a signal for the crowd to cheer. He decided that enough entertainment had been provided for the day, and besides, it was beastly hot. 'Put on some fish fry,' he said, as he walked off the dusty pitch, removing his gloves and tossing them to a minion.

'Well played, sir, well played,' said Phoni-babu, coming forward to meet him. 'That last shot of yours, it was as if Gavaskar had returned to us. What timing! Like a picture!' As a member of the Calcutta Police, Phoni-babu was practised in dealing with politicians.

The Principal was a well-built man with wavy hair and a bit of a belly. A diamond twinkled in his ear. 'What are you saying?' he said, smiling. He reached out and shook his hand. 'Where is Gavaskar, and where am I? How can I help you, dada? It's not every day I get a visit from Lal Bazaar. I am just a lowly schoolmaster. What have I done to deserve this honour? Not the chit fund case, I hope? That type of thing I have never been involved in. Whatever pictures you have seen, all photoshop.'

Phoni-babu stuck out his tongue, and bit it, indicating acute embarrassment. The greater the embarrassment, the more the tongue was supposed to stick out. He spared no effort. 'Arrey, na na sir, what are you saying? Chit fund case is at chargesheet stage, matter is very complex, where is the question of investigation? Don't worry, all that we are taking care of. This large Chinese person is my colleague, Mr Chen. We have come here about Barin-babu.'

'Sad loss,' said the Principal, 'Very sad loss. So many years he supported the party. Such a my-dear person, very genuine. All the time I would tell my boys, instead of watching item numbers, try to learn from Barin-da. Try to understand about petit bourgeoisie and class struggle, otherwise how will you call yourselves communists? Very learned person he was, always reading. Not very social. But what are you looking for here? I heard it was the thugs. Even a coin was kept on the pillow, I heard. I'm sure you understand, all news I get. I hope you're not thinking I'm a thug-fug?' He laughed uproariously. His followers, now clustered around them, joined in. He waved a humorous finger at Big Chen and Phoni-babu. 'I know you police have quotas. You must have a thug quota also. That doesn't mean you can just pick up anybody and everybody. When I go to the Education Department, do I feel like strangling people? Certainly. But does that mean I'm a thug? Everybody wants to strangle the Education Department.'

'We're checking out the thugs,' said Big Chen, butting in. The man was a talker. Big Chen hated talkers. 'The victim used to teach some boys in the evening. We're looking for them. They may have been studying at your school.'

'So many boys come and go,' said the Principal. 'We have no lack of supply. Some type of tuition so many are doing. In this district alone there are six IIT coaching centres. How can anyone keep track of who's doing what? Is it possible? Otherwise I would help you. We are always happy to cooperate with the police. You cooperate with us, we cooperate with you. If you give me the names, I can try to identify. Meanwhile, you have come all the way from Calcutta, please join us for our picnic. Jodu, is the fish fry ready? Give some to our police brothers. Look carefully, baba, select some good pieces.'

Phoni-babu looked hopefully at Big Chen. Big Chen shook his head silently.

'We're in a hurry, but you can pack some,' said Phoni-babu.

'Saala, fish is in short supply, but not for Party dada!' said Phoni-babu later, as they trudged back to their car, packets of fish fry tucked under their arms. 'Prices are growing like fire, but Party dadas are getting full supply. How much more oppression must we accept? All the what! Nonsense! Anyway, now it's very clear. We have no option. If we want to find out more about these boys, we have to go back to Motipur and interrogate the village women. Don't worry. I'll take care of them. I'm a veteran person. I've done this a lot.'

'First, let's go back to the station,' said Big Chen hastily, trying not to imagine what the boss would do to him if Phoni-babu was unleashed on the local population. 'Let the Inspector decide. If we need to, I'll do the interrogating. You can help me in case I don't translate properly.'

'Translation never brings out the real flavour,' said Phoni-babu.

8

'Sir, if you could reduce his medicine-shedicine, that also would be helpful.'

As a lifelong member of the Calcutta Club, Ganguly took great pride in his tea skills. 'Jasmine tea, or Darjeeling?' he asked. He judged people by their choices. He would pour it out for them personally, and not a drop would splash.

'How can we have anything but Darjeeling, sir?' said Agarwal, who knew his methods. 'Your Darjeeling tea is famous throughout the city. Mr Rungta had it once, and after that he was never satisfied with any other tea. Finally he switched to coffee.'

'Red Label,' mumbled Verma, but Agarwal quickly shut him up. Verma was from Delhi, where they mixed Darjeeling and Assam.

As executive assistant to Governor Wen, Ganguly was the de-facto ruler of over fifty million human beings. He bore his burden lightly. His table was bare, except for a fountain pen and a plaque that displayed a picture of Chairman Mao and the inscription 'READ LESS. WORK MORE'. In his thirty years in the civil service, he had learnt to adapt to a wide variety of circumstances. His tailor had remained the same throughout.

'Facing business problems, are we?'

'Very big problems, Ganguly-uncle,' said Agarwal, 'only bold action by Governor-sahib can save us.'

Ganguly smiled regretfully. 'If bold action is what you need, then Governor Wen may not be the right man.'

'What are you saying, sir?' said Agarwal. 'He must be a high calibre person. These days Communist Party is so competitive, and he has risen to such a high position.'

'Actually, he's fallen to such a high position,' said Ganguly. 'This Wen fellow comes from army aristocracy. His father was the Very Excellent Marshal, who performed creditably in the war against Japan. He led the amphibious assault on Okinawa. Wen himself used to be Mayor of Chengdu. Unfortunately, a shopping mall built by his nephew collapsed, slaying six. The very next day he stepped on the foot of the Young Prince at an orgy. He was still wearing shoes.'

Verma was impressed. 'Lot of action going on in China!' he said. 'Looking at them nobody can tell. I used to think they were decent people.' Not that he was entirely surprised. He'd spent a few weekends in Macau. He had happy memories of the Golden Delight Sauna, with its free service bingo and sit down showers. But that was Macau. He had always assumed that Beijing was more civilized. 'Their moral situation seems to have deteriorated.'

'Unlimited power can do that to you,' said Ganguly.

'Is Governor-sahib suffering from some kind of personal problem?' asked Agarwal. 'He seemed very depressed. One or two times it looked like he would start crying.'

He had good reason to. The flow of tribute to Beijing had not been as expected. The province was running a deficit for the third year in a row. To make matters worse, Governor Wen's economic advisors had been unable to agree on a figure for the deficit. They were busy pouring scorn on each other in a variety of public forums. The flood of investment from the Motherland had been unexpectedly delayed, as had the union with the local Maoists. The local Maoists had refused to lay down their arms, because they needed them to liberate the rest of India. They were cordial, but well-armed. Delegations of Chinese businessmen had conducted several fact-finding missions, and left very quickly. The only business booming was the arms business, where the Chinese lent money to the Maoists, and the Maoists bought weapons from the Chinese. Meanwhile, back in Calcutta, Propagandist Wang had spearheaded an ill-advised clampdown on the noodle-sellers of Gariahat, because they were an insult to Chinese culture, with their raw onions and their chunks of indigestible mutton, but the noodle-sellers had proved to be surprisingly resilient. Violence had escalated after the martyrdom of Bappa. A former mass leader had escaped from the mental institution. Efforts to apprehend her had so far proved futile. There were rumblings of discontent over the price of fish. The Kolkata Light Striders were near the bottom of the table, and East Bengal had once more been defeated by Dempo. The birth rate of Chinese immigrants was down, while the birth rate of Bengalis was up, because the Chinese were too depressed to have sex, and the Bengalis had nothing to watch on television, because of censorship. On top of everything else, their administration had been shamed administratively by the neighbouring Indians, thanks to their rapid rollout of the Smiley Drones, which kept the population under 24-hour surveillance, while broadcasting useful and uplifting slogans. Their techniques of governance were rusty, but their techniques for suppression were state-of-the-art. On the whole, there was no doubt that, despite specific instructions from Beijing, Governor Wen had been unable to move forward gloriously.

'Things have not been going well for him,' admitted Ganguly. None of this was new. He had served under many rulers. Eventually, all of them reached a steady-state equilibrium of apathy and depression. He'd been helping matters along. Whenever the Governor seemed lucid, he put more pills in his coffee. He preferred his masters foggy. They interfered less.

Agarwal was aware of this. Agarwal was aware of everything. 'Sir, if you could reduce his medicine-shedicine, that also would be helpful. He's becoming very hazy.'

'I'm sorry?' said Ganguly, raising one eyebrow.

Agarwal was impressed. You had to admire the man. Because Verma was an outsider, his lips were sealed. Such judgement. They didn't manufacture officers like him any more. Thanks to jiggery-pokery with the admission procedure, nowadays it was all somebody's nephew and somebody's grandson. Most of them were very low quality people. All they wanted was flats, premium SUVs, and American passports for their children. The Chinese ruling classes were very similar. It was true what his guru-ji said. They were all becoming one. Ganguly was different. He was old school. It was not his job to provide answers. He provided guidelines.

'Sir, is there anything you can suggest, sir?' asked Agarwal.

Ganguly sipped his tea thoughtfully. 'I find it helps if one gets to the root of the problem,' he said. 'I fear there may be a deeper malaise at work here. The thing to do is to study the psychology of the individual.'

'And who could do this better than you, sir?' said Agarwal. 'Seeing how you are supporting him on a daily basis.'

Ganguly inclined his head graciously. 'The fundamental problem facing the Governor is an absence of adequate concubines. I am unable to help, as this is not covered by service rules. Despite strenuous efforts on his own part, he is yet to find someone who can meet his exacting standards. Conditions here have demoralized him to the point of paralysis. His morale is plummeting. He needs the kind of solace that can only be found in the arms of an extremely good woman.'

Agarwal made a quick note on his phone. Concubines. Yet another commodity in short supply. He liked keeping track of shortages. Shortages meant money. Shortages to him were like sausages to a bloodhound. Onions. Baby food. Spectrum. Coal. Ammunition for the army. Rare Scottish whiskies. Antibiotics. Mosquito coils. Mustard oil. Textbooks for children. Mountain Breeze Oxygen. Red Pagoda cigarettes. The latest novel by the novelist Shankar, who was stored on a pen drive by Ananda Publishers. On the face of it, Agarwal was a mining magnate, and a steel baron, and a real estate colossus, and a retail giant, and a movie maven, and a financial wizard, and a provider of business process solutions, but what he really did was deal in shortages. Wherever supply was limited, Agarwal entered the supply chain.

'I believe you will find him much more amenable to your requests if you can satisfy him in this regard,' said Ganguly. 'In short, you need to put lead in his pencil.'

Verma was disappointed. He had thought things in Calcutta would be far more refined and cultured. Sunita was always on at him to get more cultured. He had imagined that subtle strategies and elegant sleights of hand would be involved. But this was just pimping. He did it in Delhi all the time. How was Calcutta any different? It was just the same, except that they took more time to get to the point.

'Can you give any kind of guideline?' asked Agarwal.

'Well, I imagine a trip to Eden Gardens should stand you in good stead,' said Ganguly. 'Now if you'll excuse me, I have pending files to attend to.'

'What does he mean?' whispered Verma, as they left the room. Between his accent and his vocabulary, Verma had only understood around one word in three. The man was like a cross between Shakespeare and Montek Singh Ahluwalia. His head was hurting.

'He means we have to go to Eden Gardens,' said Agarwal.

9

'Does that look like a man who would hesitate to murder someone?'

The living room was surprisingly modest, with the usual display case on one side. Instead of cheap holiday bric-a-brac and Happy Meal toys, it was full of foundation stones, souvenirs of the many projects that Bijli Bose had inaugurated. Each one was labelled neatly. Against the opposite wall was a bookcase, where the complete works of Marx rubbed shoulders with the complete works of Rabindranath Tagore. Neither appeared to have been opened much.

Bijli Bose was sitting in a richly upholstered leather armchair, perfectly still, his dhoti draped gracefully, his kurta spotless white, glass of Scotch near his elbow. He had no idea how much longer he had, so he conserved his energy for the times when he really needed it. So far, this had not proved to be one of those times. He was on the verge of pretending to be in a coma, a technique which worked well with unwanted visitors. He found most policemen deadly boring, which is why he had ignored law and order when he had ruled Bengal for all those years. Gentlemen did not deal with the police. He also preferred the proletariat to sort things out by themselves. It was the only way they could evolve. He sat staring into space, mouth slightly open, eyes slightly glazed, in the hope that the man would get up and go away. Most people gave up after a while. Inspector Li waited patiently.

'Barin Mondol was a loyal party worker,' said Bijli Bose, eventually.

'What did you talk about on the night he was murdered?' asked Li.

There was a faint flicker of interest in Bijli Bose's eyes. 'Sometimes we talked about old times,' he said. 'He would call, not me. I gave him a phone so that we could stay in touch. It was a gift. He helped build the Party in Jhargram. He guided youth in the proper direction. Ideologically he was very sound. He remained committed to the cause of global workers till the very end. But over time, it became necessary to engage with the more active elements of the proletariat, in order to suppress those who were unwilling to be uplifted. This was not his forte. He was more of a purist.'

'Was he an angry purist?' asked Li. He'd met some of those. They were unpredictable. Sometimes they stoned embassies. Sometimes they chased sluts. Usually they ended up doing hard labour.

'A sad one,' said Bijli Bose. 'He believed he could change the world through better thought processes, but sometimes this is not enough. He was an impractical idealist. Our history is full of them. From Ramakrishna to Bappi Lahiri, they have caused many problems. He reminded me a little of Charu, although Charu was completely insane. If you have access to Leader Gloogle, you should look him up. He was a big fan of China, was Charu. I was in jail with him around the time of the first war with China in 1962. We used to talk a lot. He would do most of the talking. He wanted our party to become part of the Chinese Communist Party, and to welcome the Chinese Army as liberators of the masses. I told him we should stick to discussing football and films, since in the area of politics, he was unable to talk any sense. Later on he founded the Maoists, who are now your loyal allies. Although the fact that they are refusing to come out of the jungle should be a matter of concern.'

'How about you, sir? What do you believe?'

'How are my beliefs relevant to your investigation?'

'I try to understand how each suspect thinks,' said Li.

Sexy Chen froze with horror. Distracted by his reflection in the display case, he had been adjusting his hair and pouting, but now he was fully alert. The cheering teenage girls faded into the background. He flashed a friendly grin at Bijli Bose to show that he was not part of this. He clutched Li's elbow. 'Next time they'll post you to North Korea!' he hissed.

The look Bijli Bose gave Li was imperious. 'You think I'm a suspect?'

'He talks to you on the phone. Three hours later he's dead.' said Li. 'You're a suspect. You told me what Barin Mondol believed in, and your friend Charu. What about you?'

'I believe in the upliftment of global workers, as I have always done,' said Bijli Bose, calmly sipping his Scotch. 'Besides, do I look physically capable of committing this crime?'

'Crime is never personal in India,' said Li. 'Things like alibis and fingerprints and murder weapons play no role. You have people to do it for you. In China, we put poison in our roommate's water jug, or stab our ex-wives with kitchen knives, or try to run them over with our fancy cars. It's a more intimate thing. Chairman Mao taught us the virtue of using our own hands. In India, you hire someone. If he gets caught, you take care of the family. Around here, if someone's murdered, there's only one question that needs to be answered: Who wants him dead?'

'I'm only here as an observer, sir,' said Sexy Chen, appalled. 'I can assure you that I will go back and file a report against Comrade Li, whose behaviour towards a senior Politburo member like yourself is anti-people, anti-harmony and in direct violation of the Six Excellent Ways. He used to be a good officer, but he's been backsliding recently. Overall, his attitude is poor. We of the Public Security Bureau take a very dim view of such individuals. I will recommend to my superiors that the Harmony Doctors make the necessary adjustments.'

Bijli Bose thanked him. He would have offered him a drink but he preferred not to share. He looked at Li. 'Is there anything else you would like to know, Inspector?'

'Apart from you, who else do you think I should investigate?' asked Li.

'Go and talk to the local Maoists,' said Bijli Bose. 'They're everywhere. They know everything. We used to be like that, in the old days. When I was in charge, no one could commit a crime in Bengal without asking our permission. When the criminals go out of your grip, that's when you have to worry. It's the essence of governance. Nowadays the Maoists are very similar. You should talk to Debu, their local leader. Respected war hero. Western type. Very educated. Speaks well. He was in the debating society at Presidency College. Considered good marriage material in Calcutta society. All the aunties adore him. He appears on TV regularly. Interestingly, he's a very good soldier. Fought ferociously during the assault on Patna.'

'Can I trust him?' asked Li.

'Who can trust a Maoist? Conventional armies have rules. Maoists have nothing. Everything is justified in the name of revolution. You've been in charge here for ten years. I'm very surprised you are letting them rise. You can never trust these people. Bit by bit they're building their strength. In my day, we would have...' he stamped on the ground with his foot. 'The Chinese of all people should recognize the danger. But they spend so much time making up history that they have forgotten it.'

'What about the thugs?' asked Li. 'Do you think it could have been them?'

'I have no interest in the activities of religious fanatics,' said Bijli Bose. 'I will rest now.' He closed his eyes. The interview was over.

'Are you mad?' asked Sexy Chen as they went down in the lift. 'Do you know how many pages of self-criticism we'll have to write? Nowadays they have software to check whether we're repeating.'

'You can do mine too,' said Li. 'Self-criticism is like a muscle. The more you do it, the better you get.'

'I understand you're a rugged individualist, but what was the point of that?'

'He thinks I'm a fool, and he lied to me,' said Li. 'Besides, we learnt something very vital. Something I wanted to make sure for myself.'

'What was that?'

'Does that look like a man who would hesitate to murder someone?'

As they got into the car, Li saw a slogan written on the wall across the street, crudely hand-drawn in bright red letters. All over Calcutta, the walls were covered in writing. It was how the city spoke. Like its people, it was talkative. No surface was safe. That was why no one ever bothered to paint their walls, giving the city its air of permanent decay, while at the same time communicating a wide variety of useful information. Except that this wasn't a slogan. It was a name.

'Harbin Paradise Realtors' said the wall.

That's funny, thought Li. Why would they advertise here?

10

'We of the police force always respect sentiment...'

'Now you shall die!' said the thug. 'For the glory of my goddess!' He bared his teeth in a grin as he tightened his grip on the roomal. His teeth were black and crooked. His victim was soft and plump.

'But I thought you were so friendly!' gasped the young man. 'Who knew that this was in your heart when you entered our Youth Camp? I should have listened to my mother and stayed at the Hilton!'

He rolled his eyes and collapsed, while the thug held fast to his throat. His legs twitched once, and then he was still. The thug reached into his pocket and removed his wallet. He looked up. 'I claim it's religious, but it's really a profession,' he said, looking them in the eye. 'That's how depraved we are.'

'That man looks like he's from Henzhou,' said Big Chen, pointing at the screen suspiciously. Inspector Li put a finger to his lips. The producer made low-budget anti-Japanese war movies, the kind where Chinese soldiers threw grenades up in the air to bring down Japanese fighter planes. He was hardly going to waste money on foreigners.

The thug had more to say. 'Don't judge me too harshly,' he

said, 'I'm just a product of a debased and immoral society. There are many more like me. This is what happens when you combine criminal tendencies with corrupt religious practices. Hahahaha!'

They cut to the anchor. She was dressed in a smart pink suit. Her cheeks were pale. Her hair was dark. She was perky. 'Sometimes they spared the children,' she said brightly, 'So that they could recruit them and raise them as thugs. They considered themselves to be the children of the Goddess Kali, created from her sweat. They claimed their goddess had ordered them to prey on their fellow humans. Throughout the nineteenth century, the thugs murdered hundreds of thousands of their unsuspecting countrymen, until they were temporarily suppressed by British imperialist scum. We must always remember that people from this region have a strong streak of treachery against which we must be vigilant. Thugs can typically be recognized by their yellow handkerchiefs, devotion to Goddess Kali, and a cunning and deceitful nature. Thanks to recent rumours of the resurgence of this barbaric cult, citizens travelling to Bengal or India are advised to be cautious. So enjoy your journey, help spread Chinese culture, and remember,' she smiled her dazzling smile, her eyes were like well-polished buttons, 'mixing with unauthorized strangers is one of the Thirty-seven No-Nos.'

'Well, that wasn't very helpful,' said Big Chen gloomily, as the screen went blank.

'It's all I could find,' said Inspector Li apologetically. 'But it does give us some idea. All we have to do is look for people who are deceitful and treacherous.'

'You just described 90 per cent of the population,' said Big Chen. 'No offence, Brother Phoni.'

'I'm more the loving and giving type,' said Phoni-babu, unperturbed. He was cleaning traces of blood off the end of his stick with a grimy handkerchief.

'This crime looked like a thug attack,' said Li. 'We have to consider the fact that it could actually be a thug attack. The question is, why?'

'Perhaps it was a religious matter,' said Phoni-babu, 'in which case, what is it of our father? My Big Babu was always very clear on this point. Phoni, always avoid religious cases, he used to say. Unnecessarily, too many people will get involved. We will be naked and exposed in public. One-two boys will have to be suspended. He hated suspending his boys. "My boys are very good boys", he would always tell the TV channels. Subsequently, this would be confirmed by internal departmental inquiries. A very fine man, he was. Owned three houses in Bolpur, one for each mistress. One of them was particularly talented. While singing melodious songs of Rabindranath, she could…'

'I found out about the other victims,' said Big Chen, quickly. He already knew half of Phoni-babu's autobiography, and he was trying to avoid the rest. 'They were Chinese. Minor officials. What religious problem could they have been causing?'

'More importantly, why is no one bothered?' said Li. 'I asked Sexy Chen to find out more about them. I hope he's done something. You go check out the Department of Fisheries, where the victim used to work. And let's start visiting temples. We have to find this New Thug Society, assuming it really exists. We could have asked Internal Security, but they're too busy spying on the rest of us.'

'36, Elgin Road,' said Phoni-babu.

'Excuse me?' said Li.

'The New Thug Society is at 36, Elgin Road,' said Phoni-babu. 'Everybody knows that. It's their registered office.'

'They have a registered office?' asked Li.

'Certainly,' said Phoni-babu. 'All such organizations have one. They should be having bank accounts also. Possibly visiting cards.'

'These Indians are unbelievable!' said Big Chen.

'Be nice, Chen,' said Li. 'Different people are different. They eat fish heads, we eat pig ears.' He turned to Phoni-babu. 'You mean to tell me that the organization that has murdered five people has a registered address? Do they also have a website?'

'Naturally,' said Phoni-babu. 'How will they recruit otherwise? Clearly you have not understood how religious people work here. They are a vital component of society. They are protecting the sentiment. Very often, evildoers are hurting the sentiment. At such times, they do police case against the evildoers, saying kindly take action, otherwise due to our pain we may be unable to control ourselves, resulting in destruction of public property, injury of public, or even death. We of the police force always respect sentiment, and arrest the evildoers whose black tongues are forcing others to create law and order situation. Their leaders are well-respected in society. Chief ministers have tea with them. Police Commissioners hold open their car doors. Senior journalists interview them, and help us to understand their views. Damage or injuries which occur due to outbreak of sentiment are never mentioned. It's only right and proper. It's a question of secularism. True secularism means that we respect every sentiment, without any prejudice. Some of them become ministers. They are able to buy good positions. They can afford it, because they collect money from local shopkeepers to prevent unnecessary mishaps. Although I must admit Amalendu Lahiri is not like that. He is more the intellectual type. He is the leader of the New Thug Society. Very fine man. Plays golf every Saturday. And what language he speaks! Such command he has! His language is what makes him a leader. After the editor of *Desh* magazine, it's him.'

'Since you like him so much, you should come with me,' said Li, 'at least one of us won't be thinking he's a piece of shit.'

His phone rang. It was Gao Yu. She had cut her hair short. It showed off her slender neck. She was angry. 'You think you're so clever, don't you?'

Was she drunk? He couldn't tell.

'A little,' he admitted.

'But not clever enough to keep me. I'm a genuine treasure. Everyone says so. You know that, right?'

'I do,' said Li. He knew enough not to hesitate.

'Do you ever wonder whether he treats me well?'

'Does he?' asked Li.

'Like a queen mother,' she said, giggling. 'Isn't that great? I never got to be the class flower. I never even finished school. But now I'm queen mother! Aren't you happy?'

'I wish you well, Gao Yu,' said Li, with a touch of formality, 'But I have to get back to work now.'

'Did you expect me to live on buns and water?' demanded Gao Yu. She was unpredictable. Life with her had been like walking on eggshells. 'Just because it doesn't matter to you, nobody else should care?'

'You shouldn't drink so much,' said Li, and disconnected. He pressed the button gently. I should have said something about her hair, he thought.

The boys were watching him sympathetically. They respected him tremendously for having such a hot ex-wife. They knew most of the details. It was only a matter of time before they started offering advice. It was at times like this that he needed to be businesslike. He sprang out of his chair and put on his hat. He was light on his feet, thanks to his father. His father used to be a boxer at the old Bison Club, a Beijing brothel that did boxing and betting on the side. It was a strange combination of fights and floozies, and his father had felt the shame most keenly. But he had always done his job, which was boxing. He had always put on a good show. He had passed on a few tips to his son, standing there panting in the back alley after fights, sweat pouring down his body, reeking of spilt beer and cheap perfume. He had planted in his mind some thoughts. He had shown him some moves. He had also told him to stay away from brothels, which Gao Yu had found extremely funny.

'Come with me,' he told Phoni-babu. 'We're going to Elgin Road. Chen, you take the Department of Fisheries, where the victim used to work. And for God's sake tell Sexy to stop singing in the mirror and go talk to Crazy Wu, while he still has enough brain left to form sentences.'

'Yes, boss,' said Big Chen, glad he had never married.

11

> *'When we talk about strangling,
> we mean it purely in the metaphorical sense.'*

'We are now entering Elgin Road,' said the car. 'The name Elgin is synonymous with the destruction of historic monuments. The father dismantled the Parthenon, while the son razed the Forbidden Palace. It is presumed that the family had no further issue, as most other irreplaceable landmarks across the world remain intact.'

ZAF Lounge flashed by, followed by Chaska Café, Desi Cuisine, Cream Centre, Nick 'N' Nack, Juicy Fresh, and the New Saurashtra Nimki House in quick succession. Like the rest of Calcutta, there was no lack of eateries on Elgin Road. It was the main reason why Bengalis had no money. There were a few other establishments in between the eateries, such as the Netaji Research Bureau and the Catholic Mission High School, to provide them with customers. Apart from this there were several malls, filled to the brim with more places to eat in, and the dilapidated husk of an abandoned bookstore. 'Crossword' said the sign. It hung crookedly from one hinge.

The car stopped in front of a simple three-storeyed building with bilious green window shutters and bougainvillea on the balconies. The walls might once have been pink, although most of them were now covered in slogans. 'The sun moves around the earth,' said one. 'Tank Man was executed!' said another. Along one entire side, covering it from top to bottom, was a crudely drawn pig smoking a cigar.

The front door was almost flush with the street, just a couple of steps between them. The steps were provided for public seating. Young men often sat there discussing heroines and football. Every house in Calcutta had them. It was a matter of civic duty. A brass plaque on the door said 'Amalendu Lahiri, BA, MA, LLB. Convenor, New Thug Society.' There was no power, as usual, so Li knocked on the door. 'Softly!' said Phoni-babu. 'It's afternoon, you might wake him up.'

The man was a pillar of society, judging by Phoni-babu's reaction. Li knocked harder. He drew his revolver. 'How about this?' he asked. 'Do you think this will wake him up?'

The door opened before Phoni-babu could reply. A slim, dark woman in a faded cotton sari opened the door. Her face was thin. She looked hungry. 'You've come to meet babu?' she asked softly, hardly glancing at the revolver. She was used to men with guns. Li nodded, and smiled, not wanting to scare her, and she let them in through a dark, narrow corridor. The walls were lined with oil paintings of men with moustaches. 'Ancestors!' whispered Phoni-babu. She led them to a room on the left, cut off from the rest of the building. 'These are his chambers,' explained Phoni-babu, 'they can't let us into the house, because they don't know what caste we are.'

'Maybe I should go inside and look for him,' said Li.

'Please sit down, sir,' said Phoni-babu. 'Read one of these legal magazines. He is a high person in society. Everyone in his family held good positions, except for one nephew, who became a tabla player. Bhobanipur public is very ferocious. For over one hundred years they have been producing homemade explosives. You'll cause an incident.' They sat down in front of the imposing desk. The desk calendar was three years old. The chairs they were sitting on were simple and rickety. The chair on the other side was a monument in leather, with a small, grubby hand towel draped over one arm.

'So a lot of potential recruits live in the neighbourhood?' said Li.

'Is this any way to talk?' said Phoni-babu. 'Please don't forget to namaste when he comes.'

The hungry woman brought them cups of tea. Li took a sip. It was terrible, like all the tea in Calcutta. They drank so much, and knew so little. It was odd that they were so useless at it, given that there were more tea shops per square foot here than any other place on the planet.

A tall man in a spotless white kurta stepped in. The border of his dhoti was intricately embroidered. His hair was silver, and back-brushed smoothly, and he held a silver-topped cane in one hand. Li wasn't worried. He was better armed. Phoni-babu stood up, rubbing his hands. 'Sorry for the disturbance, sir, we had one-two questions,' he said. 'Please don't mind.'

Amalendu-babu settled down in his chair, waving for Phoni-babu to sit too. He smiled at the two of them.

Amalendu Lahiri had hated the Chinese ever since his foot had been crippled by a Chinese foot massager, which was why he always carried a cane. He had watched the Chinese cancer eat away at the heart of his nation, bit by bit, inexorably, until one day it had eaten his foot, at which point he had stood up on one leg and said, 'Thus far and no further.' All his efforts since then had been devoted to their removal.

'How may I help you gentlemen?' he asked. He was aristocratic and gracious. Inspector Li hated him on sight.

'I'm interested in the New Thug Society,' said Li, 'could you tell us something about it?'

'Could you tell me what this is about?' asked Amalendu.

Li saw no harm in it. 'A teacher in Motipur was murdered,'

he said. 'All the evidence points to a thug attack. You're the head of the thugs. You advocate the strangulation of fellow citizens. It seemed logical to come and meet you.'

Amalendu smiled and shook his head. 'This is a natural misconception. When we talk about strangling, we mean it purely in the metaphorical sense. It's true that on Sundays and national holidays, we dress up in oddly unsuitable costumes and pantomime ritual murder using handkerchiefs weighted by coins. We've been doing so for generations. We practice over and over again, in order to get the hand-movements exactly right. But this is just for physical fitness. It makes the wrists and elbows more supple. Primarily, we are a cultural organization, with some light drilling to ensure that we synchronize spiritually. We also have a sister concern, the Junior Thug Society, which works with impressionable young minds. We operate in over three thousand schools. Our main focus is the mind, with secondary focus on the body. We would never assassinate anyone, let alone an educationist. I am appalled that an educationist has been assassinated. They are like jewels.'

'Since you've spent so many years training young men to assassinate people, have you considered that someone may have actually gone out and done it?' asked Li.

'It's natural to make that error,' said Amalendu. His expression was forgiving. 'All we do is clear the pollution from their minds, and help them to think good thoughts. Modern society is confusing them. Women are a source of challenge. Technology can be distracting. Western ideas are permeating. We are waiting for the return of Goddess Kali, who will destroy all the evils that have befallen us. Once we have received clear signals that she is coming, we will help to prepare the way. At that time, naturally we will rise up and destroy all evildoers. It's our duty. But currently we are focusing on culture. In fact, the boys will be performing Tagore's famous dance-drama *Chandalika* next week, in which a low-born woman causes a lot of difficulty. The women will all be played by men. I have seen the rehearsals. They are delightfully graceful. Would you like to come and see? I can give you tickets. Only five thousand rupees each. It's at Kala Mandir.'

'Chee chhee, sir,' said Phoni-babu, unable to help himself. 'Don't ask money from the police. Even from you, this is not expected.' The air was full of sentiment. In this case, his own had been hurt. 'You can give us four complimentaries, and four more for my Big Babu. His wife is just like you, very cultured. Make sure it's first row. Last week some cinemawallah gave second-row tickets, we had to break his legs. It was very unfortunate.'

'Barin-babu was against religion,' said Li, 'He was an atheist, and he was teaching his students to think the same way. Didn't this make him your mortal enemy?'

Amalendu smiled at his simplicity. Chinese people were so linear. It came from speaking a language where each word was a symbol. There was no nuance to it, no room for interpretation. Their language affected their thinking.

'Naturally, we are against the Sickulars,' he said, 'but over time, we have managed to suppress most of them. Some of the more prominent ones have performed beautifully executed somersaults and become devotees of correct culture. The remnants are scattered and few. We don't concern ourselves with them too much. Why would lions care about the barking of a few mongrels? This is the first time I am hearing about this person. The news must have been censored. *Ananda Bazar Patrika* has been carrying a lot of blank pages lately. If anything, we should worry about you people. So many of you are Christians these days. There are over 200,000 of you in Calcutta alone. The religious and demographic characteristics are changing, which is no doubt your plan.'

'The other three victims were Chinese,' said Li, 'I don't suppose you know anything about them, either?'

'We were deeply shocked to see people maligning us in this way,' said Amalendu, 'although I must tell you there were four victims, not three.'

'My mistake,' said Li. 'The fourth victim was that officer in Sina Bank, right?'

'Actually he was a purchase manager in the Fragrant Valley Trading Company,' said Amalendu, 'but I don't blame you for being confused. An officer of your experience must be handling so many cases.'

'Can you help with some leads?' asked Li. Sometimes he pretended to be humble.

'This Motipur is in Junglemahal, isn't it? Very lawless locality. No doubt godless Naxalites would have been involved, or perhaps one of the local boys. Although I am sure the local boys there are also very good boys.'

'It's likely,' said Li. 'This place is full of them.' He handed him a card. It was screenpaper. Above his name, it flashed encouraging slogans, which changed periodically. 'Avoid feudal and superstitious practices' it was saying currently. It seemed appropriate. 'Do apply your mind to the matter, sir,' he said. 'If you come up with anything, or receive any information, let us know.'

'Certainly,' said Amalendu. 'Our loyalty to the administration is absolute.'

The hungry woman ushered them out.

'What did you learn from that?' asked Phoni-babu. He knew that Li was good at investigation. He had heard of this phenomenon. He was curious.

'I learnt that good Bengali gentlemen think they know everything, so they love correcting you,' said Li. 'It shows who knows more. And they don't feed their maids very well.'

The car was waiting. They got in. 'The locality of Bhobanipur was home to many members of the Bengali intelligentsia,' said the car, 'until real estate prices in Ballygunge went up. Those who have adorned this neighbourhood include immortal leader Netaji Subhas Chandra Bose, legendary cine star Uttam Kumar, internationally acclaimed film director Satyajit Ray, architect of the Emergency, Siddhartha Shankar Ray, Commissioner of Burdwan District, Brajendranath Dey, eminent barrister, Rajendra Bhushan Bakshi, Hindu Nationalist pioneers, Ashutosh Mukherjee and Shyama Prasad Mukherjee, melodious singer Hemant Kumar, unforgettable theatre personality…'

'If you don't shut up, I'll shoot you in the brain,' said Li. 'I know where it is.'

The car lapsed into hurt silence.

12

'In case you feel an overwhelming urge to obey her, please back away slowly...'

A famous Indian batsman was weeping on the sidelines, lying on his stomach with his face in his hands. 'Please don't make me do any more push-ups!' he sobbed.

The Chinese coach blew his whistle. 'You rise,' he said.

'I can't do it any more,' said the batsman. 'How will I lift a bat after this?'

The coach was merciless. 'You do fifty more,' he said. He blew his whistle again. This was a punishment posting for him. He had been a swimming coach. He bitterly regretted visiting the *New York Times* website during the Asian Aquatic Meet in Tokyo. He had thought no one would notice.

Similar scenes of horror were being enacted all over Eden Gardens, a magnificent stadium which had been set on fire repeatedly until they had laid the seats in concrete. Calcutta crowds were naughty by nature. Each of the Kolkata Light Striders now had an individual coach. Each was being pushed to levels of fitness he had never imagined in his worst nightmares. KLS was the sole representative of advanced revolutionary thinking in the Indian Fat Cat League. Nothing less than total domination was acceptable. There were rumours of the death penalty for failure. The authorities had felt bound to clarify and put up a one-line notice in the dressing room. 'Rumours have been circulating,' it said, 'that loss of points could lead to the execution of those responsible.' Morale, never high to begin with, had plummeted. One of the players had jumped off the team bus while it was passing through Metiabruz, near the Hooghly River, and no one had heard from him since.

Verma looked around approvingly. You had to give it to the Chinese. They knew how to get things done. 'It's about time these guys worked for a living,' he said. Agarwal found the atmosphere disturbing. Some of the players were friends. He hated to see them suffer. He waved out to one of them, who was stretched out on something that was more or less a rack.

They walked to the centre of the field, where Junior Khan and his manager were waiting for them. Nearby, a small cluster of players stood in a huddle. One of them was doing a quick spot of self-criticism. 'I didn't bowl fast enough,' he was saying, 'I paid insufficient attention to the instructions of Manager Feng. I failed to work on my upper body strength. My socks smell. I was weakened by drinking too much carbonated beverage…'

A whistle blew sharply, twice. The players re-doubled their efforts. The air was filled with moans and cries and whispers and sighs. It was like a Swedish film retrospective.

Junior Khan came forward. He knew Agarwal well. They went to the same clubs. Khan was a superstar, like his father, only more cheerful and less prone to moodiness. He didn't mind being called Junior, and readily admitted that his dad was much better. Everyone loved him, even the Chinese. They were growing quite fond of Hindi movies. Their moral fibre was weakening.

'Hello Kanti-bhai,' said Junior Khan. 'Welcome to Eden Gardens.'

'This is my partner, Verma,' said Agarwal, 'he's from Delhi.'

He cleared his throat nervously. The matter was delicate. There was no good way to tell a man who was a superstar in seventeen countries that they needed him to pimp for them. Of course, it was all for a noble cause. Lives were at stake. Agarwal had managed to convince himself that his motives were altruistic, although he was not averse to making a rupee or two if the opportunity presented itself. But how was he to broach the subject? Tact would be called for.

'So, dude, where did all the babes go?' asked Verma, precipitating matters to a certain extent.

'You mean the cheerleaders?' asked Junior Khan, genuinely shocked. He respected the girls. They were performers, just like him, and his father before him, and an integral part of the KLS experience.

'Ya, man,' said Verma, 'are they tired from all the partying or what?' He emphasized the word 'partying'. What a dickhead, thought Junior Khan. Fresh from the mustard fields. Either real estate or mining. Even the sand mafia had more style.

'The girls have just finished their reality show,' he said, 'Right now they're at army HQ in Fort William.'

'Raising the morale of the troops?' inquired Agarwal, politely.

'Being trained by instructors from the Army gymnastics team. They're on a diet of soya milk and cucumber. They're suffering terribly. We tried smuggling in some burgers the other day, but the security is way too strict.'

Agarwal grimaced. There was no doubt about it. He was being fucked by fate. His original plan had involved loitering around the sidelines, chatting up one of the girls near the water cooler during a break between jumping jacks, whisking her off in his limousine for a quick tea with Governor Wen, and then allowing nature to take its own course. Beyond that he would not go. After all, he too had mothers and sisters. But he had not anticipated that the cheerleaders would be in military custody. It wouldn't be easy to get near the water coolers in Fort William, nor were they likely to be getting many breaks.

The whistle blew again. Someone had collapsed. Orderlies, resplendent in purple and gold, ran across the field with a stretcher. The stretcher was sponsored by Samsung, and shaped like a mobile phone. They were holding it at a forty-five degree angle, for greater logo visibility. Sometimes the patients slipped off, but the sponsors never complained.

'How about parties?' asked Agarwal, clutching at straws, 'You must be having some parties?'

'There is no party except the Communist Party!' barked Manager Feng, from just behind Junior Khan's left shoulder. He was recording their conversation with his spectacles.

'That's true,' said Junior Khan. 'Frankly I'm relieved. Those parties were wiping me out. Everyone wanted to come. Nobody ever wanted to leave. It was like hosting three weddings every week. They drank their body weight in alcohol.'

Agarwal hadn't realized they were being recorded. It didn't really matter. His job was to procure a Kolkata Light Striders cheerleader as a concubine for Governor Wen, which would give him the courage to file a report about Bengal designed to petrify the Politburo, and make them less likely to respond to the insults and provocations that the Competent Authority was heaping on their heads. He liked to think of it as a peace mission.

'Come on, yaar, you must be having some private parties,' said Verma, 'otherwise what is the point?'

Junior Khan smiled and shook his head. 'Just on my birthday,' he said.

Verma was disappointed on a variety of levels. During those cold, dark nights at his mine in Chhattisgarh, as the machine guns chattered and the vuvuzelas droned, he had often kept his spirits up by thinking about the goings on at IFCL parties, where power and beauty united as one. He imagined an Elysium of perpetual spring and shady groves, with wanton foreign women, the finest liquor, and big, chunky kebabs. All Sunita ever served at parties was tiny little biscuits with mysterious blobs on them, and there were never any wanton foreign women. He had soldiered on in the jungle, bolstered by the belief that if he could just avoid being massacred by the Maoists, and continued to accumulate at a 4,000 per cent margin, one day, paradise would be his. Here he was at last, at the very gates to that paradise, and they were denying that it even existed.

'When's your birthday?' he asked, without much hope.

'Not soon,' said Junior Khan. 'Is there anything else I can help you with?'

'Say the governor of some country wants to come to a party,' said Agarwal, cunningly, 'would you throw a special party for him?'

'We would,' said Junior Khan.

'And the whole KLS team would be there? Not just the players? Some governors are very particular about this type of thing. It's a question of respect.'

'Everyone would be there,' said Junior Khan.

'If you got a request like that, how soon could you set it up?'

'Depends on when the army releases the girls. Unless some of your friends would like to come as cheerleaders? We can arrange costumes for them.'

Verma and Agarwal looked at each other. They had considered the option of counterfeit, ersatz or duplicate cheerleaders, but the Governor was bound to conduct some form of verification. It was an undertaking fraught with peril. They could very well end up assembling souvenirs in the Central Jail on Andaman and Nicobar Islands, which had recently reopened for business. They shook hands with Junior Khan, saluted Manager Feng, and walked back across the field. Near the boundary, they saw the most famous of the batsmen, half bent over, panting. His coach took the whistle out of his mouth and wagged his finger in front of his face. 'Three months, no advertising for you!'

Heartrending cries of despair followed them though the tunnel, until they emerged out into the sunlight. They decided to eschew watching cricket in future, stunned by the underlying inhumanity.

It was a quiet day at the Gardens. The broad streets around it wore a deserted look. In the distance, a column of tanks was rumbling down Red Road, where fighter jets had once landed during World War II. They were on their way to the border, which remained fluid. A Smiley Drone spotted them and flew in towards them. They were red here, to distinguish them from the yellow ones used in the rest of the country. It made them less reassuring. The Smiley Drone hovered above them, playing a Hawaiian guitar version of the timeless music of Tagore as it received instructions.

The music stopped. The Smiley Drone quivered briefly and projected a hologram. It was the head of an elderly woman with a dark, round face and wild white hair. She was glaring at them accusingly. Both of them took an involuntary step backwards.

'Attention Citizens!' said the Smiley Drone. 'An enemy of the people has escaped from the Pandit Batra Institute for the Criminally Insane! Suspect is unarmed and extremely dangerous. Answers to the name of Pishi. Frequently recites poetry. Severe allergy to the colour red. May be seeking painting materials. Reacts badly to the term "Maoist". In case of sighting, please report her to the authorities immediately. In case you feel an overwhelming urge to obey her, please back away slowly, and remember to preserve teeth by always using bottle-openers. Avoid Small Peasant Thinking!'

'Naughty boy! Don't say silly things!' said the old woman, and gave them one final glare before vanishing. The Smiley Drone flew off, seeking other people to warn, playing a cheerful tune. They stood there, transfixed, as the tune faded into the distance.

'Holy Mother! Pishi has escaped!' said Agarwal.

'Wasn't she once a great leader?' asked Verma.

'Let's not remember those days,' said Agarwal. 'All the small people were acting like big people. All the dadas were worshipping her. We feared her whims and supported her fancies. Laughing at her was forbidden. Voting for her was compulsory. The soil of Bengal is rich with the ashes of those who refused. Sometimes she wrote poetry.'

'Sounds like my mother-in-law,' said Verma.

'It's not a joking matter. She has the power to make people obey. It's a crisis situation. But perhaps everything will work out for the best. The Chinese are mighty. She's just an old woman. Her former followers are well integrated with the current financial ecosystem. Anyway, there is no point in worrying. It's in the hands of the gods. All we can do is trust in them and keep making money.'

'What do we do now?' asked Verma.

'It does not seem that finding high quality concubines in Calcutta is going to be so easy. Traditionally, all of us have faced this problem. My uncle used to go to America, and as a result he contracted AIDS. My representatives are working, but I'm feeling doubtful. I think the time has come to meet Bijli-uncle. He's a very shrewd person. He looks very quiet, but his brain is always working. That's his plus point. Perhaps he can give us some suggestions.'

'This is what we should have done at the beginning, man!' said Verma. 'I tried to tell you, but you had to be clever, didn't you? Let me go and handle, you said. What handling have you done? So far, all we've done is watch the Governor do comedy, followed by the torture of cricketers.'

'Don't worry,' said Agarwal, 'Bijli-uncle will know what to do. Besides, if we want to go for the option of engineering gadar, we require a leader with charisma. Bijli-uncle has too much charisma. He's not been using it for a long time. At one time, many Bengalis were confused. Simultaneously they were supporting Shyama Prasad Mukherjee, because of his suspicion of Muslims, Indira Gandhi, because of her resemblance to Mother Durga, and Bijli Bose, because of his resemblance to a tall leader. He never really did anything, but the possibility was always there. Perhaps he'll be willing to help us. Leave everything to me.'

'If you screw this up, I'll kick your ass,' said Verma.

Agarwal smiled fondly. So aggressive he was. 'Don't do tension,' he said, 'we just have to pick up a bottle of Lagavulin on the way.'

13

'These Chinese people have banned all the TV shows, except kung-fu-shung-fu...'

'FISH FOR ALL!' proclaimed the board above the entrance. Next to the slogan was a happy cartoon fish, leaping into a bright blue fishing boat, not in the least bit put out by the prospect of imminent consumption. The building was a square concrete block in Late Period Stalinist Ugly, typical of every building ever built by the communists in Bengal. Their only other architectural contribution had been to add touches of red to historic monuments, such as the tip of the Shaheed Minar, a large and rampant phallic symbol built to honour martyrs of the freedom struggle.

The reception was cavernous and entirely empty. Stuffed fish eyed them coldly from the walls. The centre of the room was dominated by a full-scale model of the Digha Ultra-Modern Fish Auction Centre. Stuck to it was a piece of paper with 'COMING SOON!' written on it. Construction had begun in 2010, twenty-five years ago.

Phoni-babu was peering up at a framed poster listing endangered species of fish. It was illustrated, for ease of recognition. 'Pabda, chitol, topse, tangra, koi, bhetki,' he read. 'How can they be endangered? People are buying them in Gariahat Market all the time.'

'Maybe that's why they're endangered,' said Big Chen.

'It's possible,' said Phoni-babu, 'that humans are fucking faster than fish, so fish population is not growing as per requirement. What is there left in the market? Nothing except small baby fish, that too in limited quantity. This recent craze for fish-egg pakoras may also be a factor. If we eat all their eggs, where will the new fish come from? Supply is reducing rapidly. There was a protest in our locality recently. All the local aunties were marching. They preferred to be on the streets, rather than face the anger of their husbands. We suppressed it by declaring Section 144, and conducting minor lathi-charge.'

'Maybe it's a temporary problem?' said Big Chen.

Phoni-babu ran his finger over the poster. It was caked with grime.

'No,' he said, 'this was put up years ago. Problem is not new.'

Big Chen smiled to himself. Like it or not, the old goat was learning from the boss. He had never seen him use his brain before. 'Let's go meet our witness,' he said. They were here to meet a colleague of the victim and were running late.

'Why should we go in?' asked Phoni-babu. 'He should come out. Let me drag him out by his hair and hold him from the backside. Then you poke him in the stomach with your revolver. That way we'll get quick answers.'

'Let's talk first,' said Big Chen, and walked in. The corridor was poorly lit, the floor strewn with dried rose petals from some long-forgotten VIP visit. The office was huge and empty, except for a bespectacled young man sitting at one of the desks, checking out light pornography on his phone. It was a room full of files. Files on tables, files in cabinets, files stacked on the floor. Many were damp and mouldy, held together by rotting string, and home to numerous life-forms. Others had fused into solid chunks of compressed and horrible decay. The predominant colour of the room was an indeterminate, mottled grey. Tube-lights lined the ceiling. Some worked. Most flickered. It reminded Big Chen of the Museum of Ethnic Peoples in his hometown, except with files instead of Uighur veils and Tibetan headgear.

They stepped their way through the files, careful not to get anything on their shoes till they reached the young man at his desk. He was fidgeting nervously. All his colleagues had left long ago, exhausted by a hard day's work. Their day started at 11.30 with a cup of tea, followed by the newspaper, discussion of the newspaper, speculation regarding lunch, mental preparation for lunch, lunch, recovery from lunch, discreet naps, another cup of tea, rebuttals of points made earlier while discussing the newspaper, and departure, clutching a man-purse with a plastic strap. Sometimes they had review meetings.

'I didn't do anything,' said the young man. He was curly-haired, angelic and thirsty. He was hoping they weren't here to execute him. The others were waiting for him at the bar.

'No one says you did,' said Big Chen. He sat down and offered him a cigarette. Phoni-babu grunted disapprovingly. Why don't you give him a foot massage, he wanted to say. He was against mollycoddling of suspects. The young man looked around nervously. They were indoors. 'Go ahead,' said Big Chen, 'You're a party member, aren't you?'

He had to be. It was the only way to get a government job.

The young clerk took the cigarette. Big Chen lit it for him. He took a few drags, gaining courage with every puff. It looked like he wasn't going to be executed immediately. He would be able to say goodbye to his mother.

'You shared a room with Mr Mondol, no?' said Phoni-babu, 'We're trying to understand his character. What type of character was he?'

'Didn't talk much, but overall the OK type,' said the young

man. 'Except he was always clearing files too fast, and causing pile-ups on the tables of other people. Sometimes he even carried them across, without calling a bearer. I tried to tell him this was very wrong, but he never listened. Even the union had a word with him.'

'Troublemaker,' said Phoni-babu, darkly.

'We tolerated him,' said the young man, 'at least he didn't lecture people, like Mr Sarkar in Purchase. He's like a machine. Once he starts talking about the tendencies of modern youth, you can't stop him without chloroform. Even during lunchtime he shows no mercy. If anyone was going to be murdered I would have expected it to be him.'

'This look familiar?' asked Big Chen, taking out a visiting card. Inspector Li had found it in the dead man's wallet. He pressed a corner. A little hologram appeared, and bowed deeply.

'It's him!' said the young man. 'The crazy Japanese guy. He came with a ninja. The ninja was wearing a pollution mask. The pollution mask kept talking to us, saying things like, "Please don't breathe in my face", and "Kindly kill that mosquito". The Japanese are brilliant. Everything there is automatic. They even make automatic women. Netaji had the right idea, tying up with them.'

'Well, we kicked their asses in '22, just before we kicked yours,' growled Big Chen. He'd fought in the aftermath of the Limited Nuclear Incident of '22, and seen the Japanese in action. He'd left blood on the beaches of Okinawa. He was no fan of the Japanese. This was one of the many problems with these people. They talked so much and so fast, they hardly ever stopped to think. For them, the rhythm of their words was everything.

'What did he want?' asked Phoni-babu.

'He came here to look for fish!'

They both had a hearty laugh. The Fisheries Department was the last place to look for fish. Being very literal minded the Japanese would not have understood this.

'What was he?' asked Big Chen.

'Some kind of fish trader? They speak funny, so I couldn't make out. He seemed upset. Big supply, he kept saying, big supply. Finally Barin-babu took him outside. After that, I don't know what he said.'

'Maybe he took care of him?' said Phoni-babu. 'Some small donation for his benefit?'

'Barin-da was not like that. He came back looking very worried. But he never told me anything. Next thing I hear, he's been strangled by a thug.'

Silenced, thought Big Chen. Silenced by a thug.

'Should we beat him up now?' asked Phoni-babu. 'Maybe he'll remember more.' Big Chen shook his head. Phoni-babu shook hands with the young man, smiling.

'Maybe next time,' he said, 'there's no rush. We know where you work.'

Big Chen and Phoni-babu emerged from the building to find the town of Kharagpur in uproar. The street was filled with marching people. Shopkeepers on either side were hurriedly pulling down their shutters. A few of the marchers had stopped to gawk at their car, which was parked between two rickshaws. 'Our demand must be met, must be met!' chanted the marchers, 'Break the black hands, grind the hands!' They waved their fists in the air. Some held placards with drawings of strange and impossible creatures. One of them looked like a cross between a duck and a porcupine, while another was an improbably furious dinosaur, spitting its wrath at what appeared to be an innocent baby elephant.

Phoni-babu grabbed one of the marchers by the collar, and before Big Chen could stop him, slapped him twice, once on each cheek. 'What's all this drama?' he asked. The man tried to wriggle out of his grasp. He was around the same size as Phoni-babu, but not as well fed. Phoni-babu slapped him again. The man scowled.

'It's not good what you're doing,' he said, struggling, 'I'm telling you. You better stop or I can't be held responsible.'

'Then tell me what's happening, no?' said Phoni-babu. 'Do you think I have nothing better to do than beat you up?'

'How should I know what's happening?' said the man. 'I was on my way back from office. Everyone was marching and shouting, so I joined them. In any case what is there to do at home? These Chinese have banned all the TV shows except kung-fu-shung-fu and documentaries on Shanghai Expo, things like that. How many times can a human being watch the Olympic Opening Ceremony?'

'Don't talk nonsense!' said Phoni-babu, slapping him again. Members of the surging crowd eyed him resentfully, but none of them interfered. One of them gestured at them menacingly with a placard, bearing a picture of a dishevelled witch in a crumpled white sari, holding up a surprisingly cheerful baby by the seat of its pants. But on the whole they ignored them. They were just two policemen. Everyone knew one or two policemen never did anything, so long as no one attacked them directly. If they were left alone, the protest would proceed smoothly. 'Am I a donkey or a sisterfucker?' demanded Phoni-babu. 'Something you definitely know. Pretending to be stupid?' He slapped him once more.

'It's not good, I'm warning you!' said the man, angrily, 'How can I know everything? Do I look like Astrologer Bhrigu to you? This much I can tell you, they're angry about some book. Regarding that they are protesting.'

'Are they for the book or against the book?' asked Phoni-babu, who was familiar with book-related shenanigans. They were quite common. People were equally violent on both sides, although the opponents of books usually carried more kerosene. One of the simpler ways of starting a riot in Calcutta was to utter the words 'Taslima Nasrin' in a crowded bus.

'For it, naturally,' said the man, disregarding the facts on the ground. 'Whatever little remains, they're defending. Have these Chinese bastards left us anything? Everything they've banned. But this time they went too far. They banned a book by late Sukumar Roy. They are attacking Bengali culture. Cockroach fuckers!'

'Don't kick him in the balls!' said Big Chen, but he was too late. Phoni-babu kicked him in the balls, hard. The protestor sank to the ground, wheezing.

'Was that helpful?' asked Big Chen. 'What information will you get now?'

'It was a matter of respect,' said Phoni-babu. 'The man was insulting you. We can't let the silly fuckers insult the police. Whole law and order system will collapse. In any case, why waste time on this? We were here on the Mondol case. All these cheap people will just shout a little, maybe burn a few buses, then they'll go home and watch football. Such things are common. From our side, we should go back and report our findings to the boss. After that, if you like, we can go out and educate some members of the public. That's very necessary, otherwise they become too clever.'

Big Chen gave up. They got into their car, and ordered it to drive home.

14

'It's all Brother Gucci and Sister Prada these days.'

The Doberman leaped at him the moment he stepped through the door. Sexy Chen screamed, effortlessly hitting the high notes. He covered his face with one hand and reached for his gun, knowing he was going to be too late.

The dog passed right through him, and disappeared. Sexy Chen collapsed against the wall. He took off his cap and fanned himself with it. He looked at Li, who had just stepped in, accusingly. 'This is why you wanted me to go first, isn't it?' he said. 'You wouldn't even let me draw my gun.'

'This is the Department for Cyber Security, not the hideout of Tiger Face Bo,' said Li.

'I built them too well, that's the problem,' said Crazy Wu. He was a small, bespectacled man with long hair and sallow, unhealthy skin, thanks to years of living in maximum-security basements. 'They may be virtual, but they have personalities of their own. I've tried to train them to stand and snarl, but they're too eager to tear out throats. I think they read what's in my mind. Wait a minute! I have a message coming in from the Great Firewall.' He closed his eyes, lying back on what looked like a second-hand hospital bed. The backrest reclined automatically. As far as Li could see, no levers or buttons were pressed to achieve this.

Li sat down gingerly on a broken chair. It was a large room, dimly lit. Banks of servers hummed away on one side. The other half was a jungle of keyboards, screens and cables. Every flat surface, the tables, the walls, most of the ceiling, was alive with numbers, words and images. So was Crazy Wu. Shimmering pictures and streams of integers crawled across his arms and his legs and his cheeks and his forehead, and across his T-shirt and his filthy track pants. The only static part of him was the image of Chairman Mao in a pink frilly ballet costume on his chest. In the matter of clothing, hackers were allowed some leeway.

'The 5th Rifle Division is three miles away,' he whispered, 'inform them of the mass incident, and send a drone to guide them. If they kill more than ten people, give the commander bad dreams tonight. I want him to wet his pants.'

He opened his eyes and looked at Li. He smiled. His teeth were terrible. 'What's up, Li? How's that hot ex-wife of yours? She's the queen of prettypretties! A lot of the boys want to spy on her, but I make sure they don't. It's a thing I do for you.'

'Thanks,' said Li, meaning it. 'I know how busy you are.'

'I never agreed when the Happy Cow Army decided to join the government. We're too cool for things like that. We wanted to be just like Anonymous. Our dream was to take them down one day, and be mysterious and admired and get lots of girls. We never seem to get any girls, unless we make them wear helmets. We even have Happy Cow masks, just like the V masks that members of Anonymous have. His name is Chengu and he's very cheerful and reassuring, like the characters in *Kung Fu Panda*. His appeal is universal. Who doesn't love a cow? We could have been rock stars. But the others felt it was our patriotic duty to help the rise of China. Our contribution isn't valued. Look at my condition. No one ever gives me nice furniture. I don't have cushions, or a private fridge thingie. I've always wanted one of those private fridge thingies. Gloop.'

His eyes rolled back in his head. He froze, mouth half-open. Faint tremors ran across his cheeks. The displays on his skin and his clothes kept moving, like ants marching over a corpse.

'I think he's dead,' said Sexy Chen. 'Can we go now?' He was mortally afraid of Crazy Wu. No one knew exactly what he did down here, but there were rumours. A few of the people who'd come down had emerged not quite the same. One or two were rumoured to have disappeared altogether. Since Crazy Wu was in charge of most information, it was hard to discover the truth, unless he chose to reveal it.

'Duplicate overload,' said Li.

When they had embarked on their grand mission of uplifting a nation, the Chinese Communist Party had realized that keeping an eye on a billion people was never going to be easy. Galloping disloyalty had made their job harder. Money was never a problem. They had the largest internal surveillance budget in the history of mankind. Their problem was manpower. The number of observers had increased dramatically, but so had the numbers of those in need of observation. Technology had come to their rescue. Most members of the Happy Cow Army had been duplicated and installed on machines across the country, controlled by a master brain, also duplicated for safety, which reported to The Great Firewall, who was bad-tempered and crabby. Morale in the surveillance corps was extremely low.

'They're all connected,' said Li. 'Sometimes they freeze, but it's temporary.' This was not true. Sometimes they went off in ambulances, and never came back, but Sexy Chen was nervous enough as it was.

'Holy shit,' said Sexy Chen, 'I had no idea technology was fucking our brains to such a large extent. At least the Harmony

Doctors in Beijing are medical doctors, with degrees and operating theatres and everything.'

Crazy Wu opened his eyes. 'Did you bring any chocolate? I love 5 Star. It's so chewy.'

Li pulled a bar out of his pocket. He held it out to Wu. 'Tell me about the thugs,' he said.

Wu snatched the chocolate from him and ripped off the wrapper. He shoved the entire thing into his mouth. His cheeks bulged as he chewed. For a brief moment he was happy. 'They're on Elgin Road,' he said, slightly muffled, 'which is named for the Big Barbarian.' In the history of China, there was only one Big Barbarian.

'I'm guessing there's more of them than that upper-class jerk we met,' said Li. 'He's a leader. He must be leading someone.'

Crazy Wu grinned. 'Trust you to ask the right questions,' he said. 'They're sneaky, those boys. They're good at hiding, even from me. But not as good as they think. They've been very busy recently. They're all over the city. Visiting local markets. Plenty of buying and selling going on. Quite a few cash transfers to the chief thug. The boys are doing well.'

'They've been doing well with murders too,' said Li. 'Five of them so far. Notice anything about the victims? I got this list from the Governor's office.' He handed him a sheet of paper.

Wu held it gingerly. 'Really, Li?' he said. 'Paper?'

'I'm old fashioned,' said Li.

Wu switched his spectacles on and scanned the sheet. He closed his eyes. 'Odd,' he said, his eyes still shut.

Li leaned forward. 'Tell me,' he said.

Wu held out his hand.

'You know the rules,' said Li. 'One per question. Answer the question.'

'It's not the chocolate,' said Crazy Wu, 'I can get chocolate. It's the love you show by bringing them for me personally. The other victims are too ordinary. Mid-level officers. I don't see what the thugs would achieve by killing them. They're not in short supply. We have enough mid-level officers to repopulate Tibet. Or Kashmir, once the radiation levels fall. Wait a minute! They're freaks! All of them were poor. One month's salary in the bank, no secret bank accounts. That's amazing. It's all Brother Gucci and Sister Prada these days. I had no idea we still had government officers like these. Honest men in the Party! Who could imagine such a thing?'

'Well, they're dead now,' said Li, 'so the Party is a little less honest than it used to be.'

'Well, here's the odd thing. One of them isn't dead. Or he's a very hungry corpse. He just ordered a pizza, with extra pepperoni. Not dead. At least, not yet. Your Chief Thug got it wrong.'

Li sat quietly, thinking.

'This is why I like you,' said Crazy Wu. 'You're just like a computer.'

'What about telepaths, Wu,' he said eventually. 'Have you seen any of them around lately? The Governor is terrified.'

'Really?' said Crazy Wu. He was deeply interested. 'He's scared of telepaths?'

'Only because he hasn't met you yet,' said Li.

'I can find telepaths,' said Crazy Wu, ignoring the jibe. 'If you think we need to.'

'Not just yet,' said Li.

'But the Governor is disturbed. He's serving the nation. As a true Chinese patriot, it's my duty to help him. I should do something about these telepaths.'

'Whatever you do, don't mess about with my case,' said Li.

'The school teacher?' said Crazy Wu. 'Of course not. He was a great man. A very great man. You should catch whoever did it.'

'I will,' said Li, tossing another 5 Star at Crazy Wu. 'Thanks.' Wu raised his hand in farewell, integers skittering across his palm.

Li gestured to Sexy Chen, who emerged from behind a monitor.

'These people are a dangerous element in our society,' said Sexy Chen, as they entered the elevator together.

'That's why they keep them in the basement,' said Li.

15

*'Like I don't remember you checking me
out in front of the police station!'*

Propagandist Wang's room was simple and clean, like his political views. His desk was a smooth black slab floating in mid-air, held in position by maglevs. It was bare, except for his screen, and a small hologram of the Young Prince waving benevolently. 'ASSERT SUPREMACY OVER ONLINE PUBLIC OPINION!' said the wall behind his head.

'Bijli Bose is highly respected in Beijing,' he said. 'He was our supporter from the very beginning. He helped prepare appropriate ground conditions. He was the first person to put up a portrait of Chairman Mao here, at a place called Tenali in Andhra Pradesh, in 1967. It's in the southern part of the landmass formerly known as India.'

'Who complained?' asked Inspector Li. 'Was it him or Sexy Chen?'

'You'll know what you need to know!' barked Propagandist Wang.

Wang was pissed with him. He had good reason to be. Li had caused his downfall. As the Beijing Hero Cop who had brought the Fudan University Poisoner and many other evildoers to justice, Li had once been a celebrity. Girls had mobbed him on the street. His pictures had been all over Weibo. He'd drawn the line at shirtless, although Gao Yu had been keen, and tried to ambush him with a camera on several occasions. He was living proof that the system worked, and that it had a square jaw and close-cropped hair. It was a propaganda triumph, and Wang had been in charge of the propaganda. Their stars had risen together. They had also fallen together, after Li had chosen exile over ridicule. Wang had followed him, hoping to resurrect himself by taming the wild frontier. Or raising enough money to buy back a position on the mainland. The Protectorate was full of people who were either building or rebuilding their careers. Except for Governor Wen, who had given up. Li himself was standing on the edge, thinking about it.

'I thought we got along pretty well,' said Li. 'It must have been Sexy. He even warned me he would do it. Has his loyalty been noted?'

'The problem with you is, you think you're smarter than everyone else,' said Propagandist Wang.

'My ex-wife says the same thing,' said Li, 'you should get together. Maybe you can, once you make enough money to buy a position back home. She has a penthouse on Heavenly Hilltop. The view is fantastic.'

Wang leaned back in his seat and eyed Li. He was a liability. He should have disposed of him long ago, except for the nagging feeling that some day he might be needed. Right now he was being extremely inconvenient. Propagandist Wang had plans. Inspector Li was getting in the way.

'Your brain is at the disposal of the nation,' said Wang, 'not your personal hobbies. Stop wasting time on this villager. We have more important things for you to do.'

'He's not the first victim of the thugs,' said Li. 'We should probably get to the bottom of this.'

'You're no longer on the thug case,' said Wang, firmly. 'General

Zhou and the People's Armed Police will take care of it. The thugs have been declared a threat to national security. General Zhou has been asked to investigate and suppress them, which he will no doubt do with maximum inefficiency. But things can no longer be handled at your level, which is very low.'

'They're on Elgin Road,' said Inspector Li, helpfully.

'This is no longer your problem,' said Propagandist Wang. He gazed at him sternly. Li gazed back.

'What about the teacher who died?' asked Li.

'What matters is punishment of the culprits, who are obviously thugs,' said Propagandist Wang. 'Zhou is in charge. Bullets will not be spared. The families of those shot will be paying for them. Justice will be done. You need to stop worrying about this. There's something else I called you here for. I need a small favour.'

This was a peace offering. It was a long time since Wang had asked him for a favour. A guanxi event was occurring. Wang thought he was in the gutter, but the Propaganda Department was a power in the empire, even here in the semi-digested bits.

'Sure,' said Li, feeling very virtuous. He was being sensible.

Propagandist Wang relaxed visibly. 'A mysterious anti-party campaign has been running across the city. It's causing disharmony and making me look bad. Will you find out what's going on? Technically it's not a homicide, unless you count the death of my career, but I would appreciate your help.'

'What kind of campaign?' asked Li.

'It reveals forbidden things.'

Wang dealt in broad hints and general guidelines. Providing specific information was against his principles.

'How long has this been going on?' asked Li.

'A few months. It's been increasing.'

'I'll see what I can do,' said Li.

'I won't forget this,' said Wang, 'and you forget about this thug case. And for God's sake, stop harassing senior Politburo members!'

'Don't worry,' said Li.

He checked the time on his way out. It was three in the afternoon. The Maoist commander Debu-da lived in the jungle near Jhargram. He was Barin Mondol's former chess partner. If he left immediately, he could interview him, and be back from the jungle before dark.

He walked faster.

His phone beeped as he left Writer's Building, a red-brick relic of British rule. All subsequent rulers had elected to stay there. It was Gao Yu.

'You should be careful with the women out there,' she said. 'They don't bathe much. They could have diseases.'

'I don't have time for women,' said Li.

'Ha!' said Gao Yu. 'Like I don't remember you checking me out in front of the police station!'

He couldn't deny it. Whenever corruption bubbled over, and the public was restless, the government cracked down on prostitutes, to show that they were tough on crime. It never worked. The police were rough, and few people liked it. Most of them knew they were just poor girls trying to earn a living. Li had always hated it, and never took part, but, as usual, it had been hard to ignore her. He was returning to the station and they were lined up in front of it, Gao Yu and three other working girls, on their knees. The police liked to display them in public, to show people justice in action. A small crowd had gathered to leer. Others walked past the station faster than usual, repulsed. The girls had their heads down and their faces turned away, hoping to avoid the cameras. Except for Gao Yu. She was in a flimsy nightie and Hello Kitty panties, staring up at them defiantly. Her chin was set and her eyes were flashing. Li had known instantly that he would always want to protect her. One of his colleagues had leaned down and whispered something.

'You don't have the money, you loser!' she said, and spat in his face. Li had stepped in when he raised his hand.

Gao Yu watched him remembering.

'Good times, no?' she said, grinning. 'I think you broke his jaw. But don't change the subject. You have to be careful with those women.'

'I told you I don't have the time'

'Whatever. Just remember to have lots of antibiotics,' she said. 'I have to go now. My helicopter's waiting. I got a pink one. I'm going on a skiing holiday to Wusan. Not that you care, but I could make as much as 50,000 dollars from this trip.'

Li felt a pang of sympathy for her new man. He was desperate to marry her, and bleeding cash. 'Why don't you marry him?' he asked.

'And let him do it for free? Are you kidding?'

Li couldn't think of anything else to say. 'I have to go to the jungle now,' he said.

'You should stay there,' said Gao Yu, 'it would suit you.'

16

'There was a time when people used to drop dead from cholera here like leaves from the mahua tree.'

'We no longer lurk amongst you. You can sleep without fear.'

The guide was sullen, and prone to disgruntled silences. He stomped grumpily down the narrow forest trail, never looking back. Inspector Li followed him cautiously, trying not to touch the greenery. Concrete was his natural environment. Nature made him nervous.

'It's not like he has to live in the jungle, you know,' said the guide. 'All villages are under him. He could live in any one of them. It's all theatre. When those giant foreign women come to photograph him in the jungle, it looks good. It's all about setting, that's what it is. He never admits it, though. He says the revolution is not over, he must not forget about hardship. He should live with my mother-in-law. That'll teach him about hardship.'

Inspector Li assumed that he was now in Junglemahal, an independent state within the liberated zone, covering parts of what used to be the states of West Bengal and Jharkhand. Borders here were fluid. It was hard to tell where Junglemahal began, and the Protectorate ended. For most people, it meant paying both the local police, respectfully referred to as uncles, and the Maoists, represented by local area commander Debu-da. This made it a high tax area, like Sweden. Emigration levels were high.

'Of course, it's only natural he'll do theatre. Theatre is very important to them. When they're not shooting people, they're doing theatre. Some of them even prefer theatre to shooting people. It must be because of their artistic mentality. I saw one of their plays once, about this boy Eklavya. He was one of us, a tribal. Naturally he was very good with bow and arrow. This was before the AK47 had been invented. It was the main method of killing people. He was a threat to all the young rajas, who were practising-practising all the time, but not improving sufficiently. The guru-ji of the young rajas could see that he was a very suitable candidate, and one day he would challenge the young rajas. So he asked Eklavya for his thumb and, like a fool, Eklavya gave it to him. In this play, they changed the ending, and added a twist to the story. Here he shows good sense, and refuses to give his thumb to his guru. Instead he shoots him full of arrows and chops off his head. This ending was much better. Performance was good. There was plenty of dancing, and the girls were nice. Here also, when Eklavya protects the villagers, they give him food and drink, just like we do. But the quantity was much less. Nowadays there are so many of these people, and none of them produce food. They only consume it. Sir, what can I tell you? In trying to feed them, our backside is exploding.'

They walked on in silence. Inspector Li tried hard not to think about the insects in his boots as the sweat trickled down his spine. He slapped a mosquito on his arm. They were bigger here, and sucked more blood, like high-level party members. He tripped over a root, and found himself in the middle of a clearing. 'Debu-da's office,' announced his guide, and departed in search of food.

It was a full-fledged military camp, with regulation tents in neat little rows, a small brick generator room, and a mobile rig.

Not a bow or arrow in sight. A couple of sentries in olive green sauntered up and looked him over, unimpressed by his uniform but staying sharp. He was not the boss of them. They were citizens of an allied nation. Most of their gear was Chinese, Inspector Li noted, with satisfaction. Manufactured in the jungle, under licence. They were getting quite good at it. They were giving the Indian Army a hard time, a few hundred miles away in Bihar. Geography on the Western Front was a living thing, rippling and slithering, leaving little puddles of blood in its wake. Things were much more relaxed for the Maoists here in the East, with the friendly Chinese next door. In theory, cross-border relations ought to have been marked by thigh-slapping and merriment, as they celebrated the spirit of revolutionary brotherhood together, but in practice, Inspector Li couldn't recall ever seeing much of this happening.

'I suppose Swapan-da won't do, only Debu-da,' said one of the troops.

'I'd prefer that,' said Li, 'I'm investigating the murder of a government officer who lived nearby.'

'He means Mondol-da,' explained one guard to the other. 'He was strangled last week. Mondol-da was OK. He ate very little, and never stole anything.'

They walked him to the command tent. As they approached, they could hear the funky beats of A. R. Rahman. Inspector Li was intrigued. This was an unlikely place to find a classical music fan. He raised the flap and stepped into the tent.

It was a large tent, dominated by an active-surface table with touch panels. There was a low, narrow cot on the side. On it sat Debu-da, a pleasant, open-faced man in spectacles and green fatigues. A copy of *Stardust* magazine lay next to him, featuring two identical women on the cover, striking martial arts poses. 'I'M IN LOVE WITH MY CLONE!' SAYS SHEILA, the cover blared. Sensing his interest, the magazine began to speak. 'It was a romance that began during the shooting of *Kung Fu Twins*...' said the magazine. Its voice was warm and thrilling. Debu-da hit it with the butt of his rifle, and it subsided. 'It's amazing how my clone is hotter than me, Sheila was quoted as saying...' it ventured tentatively, but Debu-da glared, and it fell silent. Its cover went blank, just the *Stardust* logo gleaming eerily in the dim light of the tent. There seemed to be a book underneath it. Was that a pig on the cover?

At first glance, Debu-da seemed surprisingly young to be such a pillar of society, until Inspector Li noticed the touch of grey at his temples. He had the easy confidence of a veteran, and an air of amiable menace.

'This is just like Agatha Christie,' said Debu-da. 'Big city cop visits innocent villagers. Do they read Agatha Christie in China?'

'We adore her,' said Inspector Li. This was true. They were mad about A-Granny back home. *The Mousetrap* had been running forever. 'And your boys outside don't look like villagers,'

'I keep them in shape,' said Debu-da, modestly. 'They say the fire inside me is gone. That's why I'm here, instead of at the Front. But I keep the boys tight. Otherwise they might get up to mischief. You know how it is. Around here, there's not much to do. I'm extremely strict. Discipline is my middle name.'

A dreamy-eyed soldier popped his head into the tent.

'Guru-ji, come join us outside, the jungle smells heavenly!'

Debu-da waved him away, smiling. 'He's in love,' he explained.

Inspector Li was happy to see romance flowering in the jungle. He hadn't been getting much himself, although one of the waitresses at the Serve The People in Chowringhee had been giving him the glad eye lately, so maybe there was hope. It was hard to concentrate, with Gao Yu calling all the time.

'What happened to the fire inside you?' he asked.

'Oh, it just went out one day,' said Debu-da, looking quite

undisturbed. 'We've been doing this for years, and nothing much changes. Patna was a bloodbath. The army boys are tougher than the poor constables we used to blow up. I was good at killing, but how much can you kill? Patna's a great prize. I understand the value of Patna. Emperors have ruled from Patna. But how much blood is it worth? "Why don't we just divide it up and settle down?" I said to my comrades one day. They disagreed. They want everything. They locked me up for a few days while they figured out what to do. For a while it looked like the People's Court, which has a 100 per cent conviction rate, but my boys were getting restless, so I was let off with some Medium to Heavy Public Criticism, along with thirteen hours of revolutionary poetry.'

Inspector Li was sympathetic. 'Reading or writing?' he asked.

'Reading,' said Debu-da. 'At least it wasn't singing. I hate those songs. I prefer Clapton.'

He was a long way from Presidency College, where the walls were steeped in history and all the girls were clever. He had been full of revolution back then. His original plan was to become a leading intellectual, but mounting injustice had transformed him from light pink to deep crimson. Later, it turned out he had a talent for jungle warfare. So here he was, in a spacious tent, a slightly exhausted leader of men.

'Tell me about Barin Mondol,' said Inspector Li.

'He was one of the few we didn't kick out,' said Debu-da. 'Usually, we drive out the babus when we take over. They go and hide in the district town, and pretend they're still on duty. That way they still get their budgets every year. No one ever comes to check. We take our share once a month, so everyone's happy. We're government servants too, in a way. A few of the stubborn ones we have to kill. Barin-babu refused to leave, but we didn't kill him.'

'Why?'

'Everyone in the village said he was steady. A few even asked us to leave him alone, which takes plenty of guts these days. He never bothered us. He lived alone, did his job, helped some kids. I first met him when we took over the village from the CPM, just before Reunion. Those were the bad old days. Now we're all brothers, of course. Bangla-Chini Bhai Bhai!'

'Bangla-Chini Bhai Bhai!' responded Inspector Li, not really meaning it. As a rule, he preferred brothers who were less heavily armed. 'What kind of person was he?'

'His theoretical knowledge was very sound,' said Debu-da. 'He spent a lot of time analyzing our missteps, and demonstrating the inherent fallacies behind our ideological assumptions. He was a solid chessplayer. We played once a week. He was a risk-taker, but also a long-term planner, which I always found fascinating. Nothing reveals character better than chess. He was very well-read. He did a lot of his reading in the old days, before you people came and banned whatever the Indian government had missed out, leaving us with romance, cricket and astrology. But he remembered a lot. He could quote entire passages from memory. I had an uncle like that, a judge of the Calcutta High Court. Complete asshole. Collector of property. He would hand out his card to anyone who owned some. "I'll get you a very good rate," he would say, "you won't have to work anymore." He was more of a pimp than a judge. Well, now that we're done, do you fancy a drink? I have Old Monk, the best alcoholic beverage on the Indian subcontinent. Our Nepalese comrades liberated the factory.'

'The last time you played chess together,' said Li, 'did he discuss anything in particular?'

Debu-da eyed him with interest. 'Trying to discover the truth, are we? You must not get promoted much.'

'Not much,' admitted Li. He waited.

'Well, he was depressed, but no more than usual. Said we were all turning into money-grubbing chimpanzees, without knowledge or culture. I said that started happening years ago, but he said that the pace was accelerating. "I've tried to be patient," he said, "but sometimes I think all of you should be destroyed." You Chinese worry a lot about angry youth, but I'm not so sure about that. It's the angry old men. Those are the ones you have to keep an eye on.'

'Has there been any thug activity around here lately?'

'I've never seen a thug. No one has. Apparently they mix in with the rest of society, pretending to be our friends. Anyone could be a thug.'

'Like the Maoists hiding in the city?'

'There are no Maoists hiding in the city. It's true that there was a time when we had infiltrated urban society at every level. We were all around you. Babloo's uncle, Chinmoy's brother-in-law, Boobli's cousin, your driver's nephew, the little boy who brings you bread every morning, the Deputy Director of the Archaeological Survey of India, the construction worker who looks too smart to be a construction worker, the Assistant General Manager (Purchase) at Mother Dairy, that nice professor who introduced you to Hemingway, the girl sitting next to you in the food court, the bearded man on the bus, even some of the younger members of Calcutta Club. But that was when the feudal reactionaries were in charge. Now that progressive forces control Calcutta, this is no longer the case. We no longer lurk amongst you. You can sleep without fear. Once in a while you can let your security guards take a holiday. No one is going to come in the middle of the night to line you up in front of a wall and shoot you.'

'That's a great relief,' said Inspector Li.

'You don't have to worry about us, truly,' said Debu-da. 'The war is over in Junglemahal, and we want to keep it that way. I love my boys. They've done enough. They want to live life now. And things have improved. There was a time when people used to drop dead from cholera here like leaves from the mahua tree.

Things have improved. About the thugs, I'm not so sure. They're the upper-class Hindu type. Their work is never finished. Driving backwards always takes more time. We want to go forward, inch by inch, and maybe kill fewer people while we do it.'

'That's why you have more time for reading,' said Li, pointing to the book under the *Stardust*. 'May I borrow that? It looks interesting.'

Debu-da hesitated. Then he shrugged. 'Why not?' he said, grinning.

The book had a picture of a pig smoking a cigar. *Animal Farm*, said the cover.

17

*'Morning-evening I'm serving the public,
stopping only for meals.'*

Geju-da's home was opulent, with drones buzzing in every room. Apart from several chandeliers and an auto-remould sofa set, the living room was dominated by two gigantic portraits, in intricately carved golden frames. One was of Governor Wen, in a dark blue suit, looking depressed, while the other was of renowned cine star Mithun Chakravorty, in a flowing robe of crimson. He had one hand raised in blessing. His smile was heavenly.

'These are remote-controlled paintings,' said Geju-da, 'in order to preserve flexibility.' He pointed at the portrait of Governor Wen. The painting floated off the wall, performed a quick horizontal flip, and reattached itself once more. It was now a portrait of a wild-haired elderly woman with accusing eyes. 'That's Pishi,' explained Geju-da. 'Time to time she also comes to power. She's not easy to suppress. You kept her in a mental hospital, but recently she escaped. Or perhaps they were too scared to keep her, and simply allowed her to leave. That's very possible. Chinese may be strict, but Pishi is Pishi. My house can adjust, depending on current administration. All latest technology.'

Geju-da was a wiry little man in a simple white bush-shirt and tight black trousers. He was in his thirties. The top three buttons of his shirt were open, displaying a thin, smooth chest covered in gold chains. He was sitting on a medium-sized throne. His guests were on the sofa, which was massaging them discreetly.

'What about Mithun-da?' asked Phoni-babu. 'Who does he turn into?'

'There's something called loyalty in this world,' said Geju-da. 'Where is the question of replacing him? He is in our hearts forever! Don't mind, but what kind of third-class person are you to suggest such a thing?'

'Oye, oye, oye!' said a small, dark drone, hovering near his left shoulder. It threateningly extruded what appeared to be a syringe, along with a small laser. Blue flashes of electricity crackled all over it. 'Sillyfucker! It won't be good, I'm warning you!' said the drone. Geju-da held up his hand. The drone grew still, hovering in mid-air.

'Does he do kung-fu?' asked Big Chen, keen to defuse the situation.

'He does everything-fu,' said Geju-da. 'He is multi-talented. He can do Madrasi. He can do Marwari. He can portray divinity. He can portray criminality. He can encourage children on television to reveal inner talent. He is an accomplished dancer of the disco. He achieved notable success as a hotelier. If you like, I can introduce you. But tell me, how can I help you gentlemen? I wasn't expecting you, Phoni-da. No financial question has cropped up, I hope? Our rate has been fixed. Supply is regular. Suddenly, what happened?'

'Arrey, no, no, what are you saying, Geju-babu?' said Phoni-babu. 'Your dealing is very clean. Problem is, our boss is very difficult. He wants us to meet everybody involved in this case. It's like some sort of obsession with him. But now that you've met us, our job is done. Give us some tea-shea, one-two biscuits, and we'll be on our way. You must be busy.'

'What keeps you busy?' asked Big Chen. Li had asked him to find out more, and given him some questions, which he intended to ask. Phoni could kiss the man's feet as much as he liked. 'What do you do exactly, sir?'

'This and that,' said Geju-da, modestly, 'here and there.'

'Let's respect his privacy,' urged Phoni-babu. 'What kind of society will we be without privacy? Our freedoms must be protected. Police should not get into everything.'

'I don't mind telling you at all,' said Geju-da, 'it's a matter of pride, what I do. I'm serving society. See, sometimes people have requirements. If there are too many people to fulfill these requirements, they get confused. For example, say you are building a house. For the house you need cement. If too many people are supplying cement, lot of time goes in selection, trying to assess price, quality and other such factors. House building gets delayed. Better to go through one person. Wastage of time is less. Efficiency is more. In other cases, the requirement is people. Our village is full of unemployed youth. World is full of requirement. That's why, in every locality, the Party has nominated one person to take care of all the requirements of the public. Out here, I am that person, thanks to previous good work. Sometimes people resist, and we have to break their legs, but we always take them to the hospital afterwards. Hospitals are very cooperative.'

'Are there any specific areas you work more in?' asked Big Chen.

'Economy is not very developed here,' said Geju-da. 'During the time of Bijli-da, union was very strong. First they targeted big companies, big companies left. Then they targeted small companies, small companies shut down. After that they started chit funds.'

'What's a chit fund?'

'It's a method for collection and redistribution of small savings,' said Geju-da. 'Personally, I avoid it. Public gets angry, and they know where I live. Police charge more to beat them up. Plus, it's a question of humanity. I have seen people suffer heart attack due to pressure. Still, it's a sacrifice from my side. Maximum money is in this line. Instead, I am contributing mainly in the service sector, and in small-tiny local requirements, like house building, betel-nuts, and threatening.'

'You've come here about Barin-da, isn't it?' he said, coming to the point. 'Ma Kali, I swear, I had nothing to do with it. He was our respected Mister Master. Very genuine person. Always reading all the time. Never caring about money. Talking only when required. Such people I respect a lot. I always tell my assistants, unfortunately you are all like me, but you should try to be more like him. None of them ever listen, of course. Their affection for me is too much.'

'What about all these local boys?' said Phoni-babu, 'I hear you're supporting so many of them. That's also a social service, Geju-babu. Tell him about that.'

Geju-da smiled modestly. 'In this case, my social service is combined with business requirement. I need a distribution channel. I hire boys to do my distribution across Calcutta.'

'What do they distribute?' asked Big Chen, guessing drugs.

'This and that,' said Geju-da. 'Small items. Margins are very low, but somehow we all survive.'

Judging by the size of his house, some were surviving better than others. 'Did any of his students work for you?' asked Big Chen. 'One of them told my boss that he does.'

'It's possible,' said Geju-da, 'but how would I know? I'm very professional. Personal lives I don't interfere with. It becomes a question of individual liberty. Besides, where is the time? Morning-evening I'm serving the public, stopping only for meals.'

'Geju-babu, don't mind,' said Phoni-babu, 'but one question I have to ask you. If your boys are getting educated like this, won't they get jobs? Barin-babu was doing education. Isn't this bad for your business? In your place I would be upset.'

Geju-da laughed. 'Jobs! What jobs? We haven't had any jobs here since 1986. Why he was teaching them, he only knows. Or knew, I should say, since he has left us. From my side, I have no complaints. All the boys are very good boys, doing very well. Customers are fully satisfied. Nowadays, they are even selling to our Chinese maliks. My business is getting international flavour.'

The man knew more, but he wasn't going to tell them. He could keep blathering like this for hours. Big Chen lacked the patience of his boss. Not that his boss was always patient. He had a fine judgement regarding when to listen, and when to draw his gun.

'I'm going to need a list of your boys,' he said, as he got up to leave.

'Certainly,' said Geju-da, 'we are always there for you. If you have any other sort of local requirement, do let me know.'

'We always do,' replied Phoni-babu.

18

'Like a girl who can sing?'

Agarwal ducked, and the bomb flew over his head, exploding against a lamp post on the far side of the street. He scrambled to safety behind the smouldering hulk of a recently burnt car. A bullet smacked into the fender. He hit the ground, face down, right next to Verma, who was feeling homesick for Chhattisgarh. The bomber backed away to his group. 'Sot! Sot!' said his comrades. They were standing in the middle of the street, shouting slogans and curses, firing away. Their rivals were at the far end, trading bullet for bullet, bomb for bomb, and insult for insult. The air was thick with explosions and curses. It was like Diwali with an X-rated soundtrack.

'Motherfucker!' said Verma. 'I thought leaders lived here! Where the hell are the water cannons? What about tear gas? Is there no law and order or what?'

'Violence is very democratic in Calcutta,' said Agarwal, 'you can be blown up, burnt, shot, stabbed, strangled, attacked with a chopper, or bashed with a brick anywhere in the city. Real estate value is never a factor.' There was an explosion just behind them. They clutched each other like lovers. They felt each other up cautiously, to make sure they were both in one piece.

'Same Same CPM!' roared the boys at one end, who were

indistinguishable from the boys at the other. 'SAME SAME CPM!' They were all thin, dark and wiry, in tight jeans and bright shirts unbuttoned to the navel, their concave chests bared to the world fearlessly.

'Is it Tuesday?' asked Agarwal. 'I'm so sorry, I forgot that it's Tuesday.'

'Why are they doing gadar in front of Bijli Bose's house?' asked Verma. 'And who's fighting whom? Didn't the CPM wipe out everyone years ago, thanks to support from the chinkies?'

'They did,' said Agarwal. 'It's Tuesday. Every Tuesday, they play Exhibition Match under his balcony. It's similar to the arrangement with the Pope in the Vatican. They do double role. Ruling party, opposition party, both are played by them. Sometimes he comes out and watches. It reminds him of the old days.'

Bijli Bose's house was twenty feet down the road, pale, pink and two-storeyed, with bright blue window shutters. It was the only house with nothing written on the walls. His neighbours were not so fortunate. Their walls had a lot to say. 'MAY A THOUSAND SWISS BANK ACCOUNTS BLOOM!' said the wall next door. 'REMEMBER MAY '35!' said the wall across the street. 'LEARN THE TRUTH FOR FIFTY RUPEES!' said another. The guards in front of his house were peering over their sandbags, watching the show. One of the players charged, cheered on by his comrades, until he was blown off his feet by a bomb. Two of his comrades scuttled across and dragged him away, bleeding. There was a brief lull. It was time for some verbals.

'I'll play harmonium with your grandma's cunt!' promised someone from behind a burning bus.

'I'll shove my dick in your father's ear!'

'I'll stuff a brinjal up your grandfather's ass!'

'I'll play tabla on your mother's tits!'

Verma was on his stomach in the gutter, otherwise he would

have clapped. Punjabi was a good language for abuse, but the Bengalis were second to none. It was the poetry in their souls. He turned his head to look at Agarwal, who lay face down, perfectly relaxed, like a man taking a break during yoga.

'How long will this go on?' he asked. Agarwal turned over on his back and looked up at the balcony.

'So far he's not come out, and it's getting dark. He pours his first drink at sunset. That way he's very particular. According to me it's almost over.'

Soon the street was silent again, except for the groans of the wounded. The players dispersed, firing off the occasional curse to deter pursuit. Once the coast was clear, the local police arrived, and courteously escorted them to Bijli Bose's doorstep.

To the extent that Bijli Bose demonstrated any facial expression, he demonstrated some when he saw Agarwal. There was the faintest twitch of a smile on his lips, and a tiny flicker in his eyes. 'Hello, Kanti,' he said, his voice thin, but surprisingly clear and strong. 'Is your father well?'

'He's fine, Bijli-uncle,' said Agarwal, 'you're looking fine yourself, I must say.'

Bijli Bose held Agarwal Senior in high regard. During his annual summer holidays in London, he had always ensured a constant flow of fine food and rare beverages. 'Let me repay some of his hospitality,' said Bijli Bose. He raised a finger and an elderly Bengal Club bearer shimmied in, tightly breeched and whitely jacketed, complete with cummerbund and pantomime turban. Every member who completed fifty years at the Bengal Club received an armchair and a bearer free, to help create a more club-like atmosphere at home.

'I see you got caught in the Exhibition Match,' he said, once they all had a drink in their hands. 'They're useless, these new boys. Lack of competition has made them soft. We should have preserved some competitors. The Maoists are much tougher. If it wasn't for the Chinese, they would have taken over by now.'

'It's funny you should mention Maoists,' he said, 'my friend here has a factory in Chhattisgarh.'

Bijli Bose turned his head to look at Verma. 'Our boys must look very incompetent to you.' Verma couldn't deny it. They were just amateurs with extensive vocabularies. The Maoists would have wiped them out in minutes.

'Uncle, situation has deteriorated,' said Agarwal, 'the Competent Authority in India is trying to cause another war. After half the country was wiped out last time, you would think he would hesitate, but he is bold and visionary, thanks to IAS training. He is continuously insulting the Chinese. Naturally their sentiments are getting hurt, and they are launching submarines. Currently India has no submarines, but the repair work is receiving top priority. Files are moving like lightning. Before full drama develops, we require Governor Wen to take some small action, but he is suffering due to lack of good concubines. Ganguly-da was saying he requires some type of special encouragement or stimulus.'

This confirmed what the Indian PM had told him. She was a bright girl, full of good ideas. She came from a good family. Her nose was just like her grandmother's. Based on her information, he had set wheels in motion. He had also given her some excellent advice regarding Taiwan. His opinion of the Competent Authority was not as high as Agarwal's. He was no admirer of Indian babus. Most of them would sell their mothers for a bottle of Blue Label. Few of them could ever make out whether it was genuine.

'I'M GOING TO GET FUCKED, UNCLE,' said Verma, who always spoke loudly to old people.

'Perhaps you could give the Governor some kind of tasteful, cultured offering?' suggested Bijli Bose.

'Like a girl who can sing?' asked Verma.

'I was thinking more along the lines of a Ming Dynasty Noodle Bowl.'

Agarwal tried to hide his disappointment. Matters had gone far beyond noodle bowls. Bijli-uncle was obviously out of touch when it came to the Governor, whose appetites were genuinely disturbing.

There was a commotion in the adjacent room. 'Red Lebel ti?' said a loud female voice. 'Wans more?' A fine china cup came flying through the open door and smashed against the wall, followed by a saucer. They heard the sounds of a grown man sobbing, dry, hacking sobs from deep within. Agarwal looked at Bijli Bose. There was an expression on his face that he had never seen before. It was fear.

'What was that?' asked Agarwal.

'Just the television,' said Bijli Bose. His face was ashen.

A little old lady in a white sari burst into the room. 'What's happening is not good, I'm warning you, Bijli-da!' she said, 'You're insulting me with Red Lebel? No, no, sit where you are, don't stand up. Sit, I'm telling you! If you fall down and fracture your hip, who will have to look after you? Me, who else? And who are these characters? That one looks like a Panjabi.'

'Pishi!' said Agarwal.

Pishi ignored him and glared at Verma. Verma found himself unable to move, transfixed by her gaze. She was radiating gigantic concentric waves of insanity and power. Bijli Bose shrank visibly in his chair. She pointed a trembling finger at Verma, roughly aimed at his crotch. 'Your pantaloons!' she said. 'Remoobh dem!'

Verma was wearing red trousers, partly in honour of Bijli Bose, and partly because of his sharp fashion sense. He unbuckled and unzipped meekly, and removed his trousers. He rolled them up and tucked them under his arm. Disobedience was out of the question.

'Good boy,' said Pishi. 'You must be thinking, what is Pishi doing here? But Pishi is ebhrywhere! Pishi is in ebhrything! Nothing escapes eye or ear of Pishi. I was in the place for mad people, because I was phed up of all these naughty boys, always doing nonsense bloody. I was resting. Then one day I thought, enough of resting, now I must save the country, everything going to jahannum. "Nonsense boys, open the door," I told the guards. They opened the main gate and released me, saluting. I came straight to Bijli-da. Although we are enemies, he is fond of me. I'm like his younger sister. Isn't it, Bijli-da?'

'I feel guilty because we smashed her head when she was in the opposition,' said Bijli Bose tremulously. 'She was in Belle Vue Nursing Home for a week. Secretly, I always felt great affection for her, because of her fighting spirit.'

'I also feel affection for you, dada,' said Pishi fondly, pinching his cheek, 'even though you're a looj character, always drinking.'

Agarwal folded his hands. 'Pishi, please help us. We are good boys, requiring your help. Only you can do it.'

'Ey Panjabi,' said Pishi, 'you come over here.' Verma shambled across obediently, and squatted next to her, so that their eyes were level. She felt his bicep. 'Nice, strong boy you are,' she said. 'Are you a cricketer? My Light Strider batsmen are ooweek, because of torture by Chinese.'

'I can learn very quickly,' said Verma, 'bas, just give me a bat and I'll start practising.'

'First let me solbh your problem,' said Pishi, 'that's my main job, I solbh all the problems. They can challenge me, but I am nebhar difited. Sitting in the next room I could hear you. My hearing is bhery good, because ebhryone was always plotting against me, and whispering. What is the use of whispering? You think I am a phool? Pishi can hear ebherything! Your problem is with gobhorner, no? That gobhorner is a looj character. Maximum Chinese are like that. I know what to do.'

She whipped out a card from her blouse, and gave it to him. She looked bashful for a moment. 'I pheel shy because Bijli-da is a senior person,' she said. She leaned forward and whispered in his ear. Verma listened to her, growing progressively paler. After she had finished, Pishi gave him a push. 'Now go, go, phinish!' she said, 'I hate westej of time.'

They backed out of the room and slipped down the stairs. Outside, the street was deserted. The players had gone home, or to the hospital, as per requirement. Agarwal took the visiting card from Verma's trembling fingers.

'POLTU-DA's WILDLIFE SUPPLY,' it said, 'FULFILLING ANIMAL REQUIREMENTS SINCE 2021.'

'What do we have to do?' asked Agarwal. 'Some kind of 420 business?'

'I'll tell you on the way,' said Verma, weakly, wishing he had listened to his father. 'Sanju-beta, do your business anywhere,' his father had said, 'but never go to Calcutta.' He was beginning to see why.

19

'It was a cartoon pig smoking a cigar.'

'I was born in the Year of the Pig,' said Governor Wen, 'that's why I'm so loyal and lovable.'

Inspector Li smiled encouragingly, while making sure his hat recorded everything. Gao Yu loved intimate glimpses of the rich and famous. He took care not to make any sudden movements. The Governor was looking fragile. Fear filled his eyes. Sweat beaded his forehead. Sensing this, his chair extruded an arm and gently dabbed him with a cologne-scented tissue. It was designed to cater to his every need. 'Must this too be done by a machine?' wailed the Governor. 'Can I not feel the gentle touch of fingers on my forehead?'

Li was sitting opposite him, at a huge mahogany desk, in one of the many cavernous rooms in Raj Bhavan, the official residence of the Governor of Bengal since 1905. It was modelled on the home of George Nathaniel Curzon, 1st Marquess of Kedleston. Give the British credit, he thought, they knew how to build to impress, with their balustraded balconies and their grand arched gateways and their ornamental bird-cage elevators. Not to mention the thirty-acre compound guarded by lions and sphinxes. It wasn't Xhongnanai, but it had a style of its own. More than the fear of laser rifles, what really cowed you down was the fear of not holding your teacup properly, or causing too much of a splash when you dropped the sugar cube in.

'It was a cartoon pig smoking a cigar,' said Governor Wen. 'It was on the wall near the arched gate, facing traffic. Do you think it was some kind of affectionate tribute?'

'Pigs mean different things to different people,' said Li, carefully.

'It's an insult!' hissed Propagandist Wang. 'Do you see now why I asked you to look into this? Even the Governor is being targeted. Forget what kind of person he is. He is the symbol of the Motherland. When you insult him, you insult Mother China!'

Governor Wen eyed Wang suspiciously. It seemed that there was disrespect in there somewhere. But he had bigger problems to worry about. 'What do you think, Li?' he asked. 'Where did this pig come from? And is it insulting me?'

'It probably is,' admitted Li.

'Unless I execute the culprits, this will be seen as a black mark,' said Governor Wen. 'As it is there are so many mass incidents. These people are unmanageable.' He shuffled the papers on his table hopelessly. 'Students are protesting because their results are delayed. Intellectuals are protesting inhuman torture in Palestine. Tiljala is protesting the death of Jagannath, alias Mandela. Taxi drivers are protesting diesel prices. East Bengal supporters are protesting the lack of hilsa. Mohun Bagan supporters are protesting the lack of prawns. Why does everyone protest so much? How is this the City of Joy? Where did all the joy go?'

'If it reaches a certain scale, they get a holiday the next day,' said Li. 'It's called a bandh. People protest injustice by sitting at home and watching television.'

'If everyone's sitting at home, who's burning all the buses? Don't they burn buses, and those cute tramcars that move so slowly?'

'They take turns, sir. Some of them burn buses, while the others rest at home. Everyone does their share. It's a true communist society.'

'What do these barbarians know about communism?' sneered Propagandist Wang. 'They're too busy worshipping primitive idols like Durga.'

In an attempt to educate the masses and display a keen understanding of local culture, Propagandist Wang had recently launched the slogan 'CCP is the true Durga of Bengal People!' with a vibrant, evocative multimedia campaign. Airstrikes had been required to suppress the subsequent riots. It was a sore point with him.

'They hate me, don't they?' said Governor Wen. 'Even though I've spent so much time weeding out the undesirable elements, the rest of them still don't give me affection. I'm starved of affection, Li. It's not just the natives. Even our own people have been disrespecting me. I distinctly heard someone call me a fat fuck at the Junior Civil Servants Quarterly Happy Evening. Other officers looked at me with anger and loathing. I saw them whispering. Several people stepped on my foot at the buffet. Where does this hatred come from, Li? All I feel for them is affection. My heart is as big as a mountain. All I want is that they should move forward harmoniously and fulfil the Chinese Dream, while keeping me informed about undesirable elements. Despite this, unhappiness is spreading. Even the elite are infected—I noticed at a recent cocktail party at Ballygunge Circular Road, they were disturbed and unhappy. On top of this, we have telepaths. From India. The bits of it that we didn't drop bombs on. We do have telepaths, don't we, Propagandist Wang? You mentioned them at our last meeting. I was paying attention.'

'They claim that it was we who attacked their telepaths, as a result of which many are now out of action, and some are missing,' said Wang. 'We believe this is a filthy trick which deserves a proud and powerful reply. Their telepaths are not missing. They have crept across the border to attack us. This is an act of war. I have proof.'

He pressed his ring. An angry man in spectacles materialized. His hair was white. His jacket was bulging. Above him, and slightly to the right, four small floating heads appeared. 'Is the nation being shamelessly betrayed?' demanded the angry man. 'Are we all victims of a massive conspiracy? Was there really an attack on our telepaths, or are we, once more, being duped, by a government that doesn't really care?'

One of the smaller heads spoke up. 'Kindly don't say this, sir,' he said, 'as it is our officers are nervous, because the telepaths are reading them like newspapers. Such types of allegations are unnecessarily hampering their morale. They are unable to perform properly.'

'Please, let's not play the morale card,' said the angry man, expanding visibly, 'the nation wants to know one thing, and one thing only. Is there a mass conspiracy? Who else is involved in the cover-up? How much longer can you continue to fool people? Because you know, you can fool some of the people some of the time, but you cannot fool all of the people all the time. Why don't you just come out and admit it? These telepaths are not in hospital. These telepaths have not disappeared mysteriously. Right now, as we speak, these telepaths are secretly training at a secret training camp, getting ready for a foolhardy and poorly planned attack on Chinese territory. Ladies and gentlemen, the question facing us all today is this—are we, once more, being dragged into a needless and suicidal war, by a callous and insensitive government?'

He glared at the camera accusingly. They leaned back, transfixed. The words 'GOVERNMENT'S SECRET WAR?' appeared above his head, changed colour several times, and flashed menacingly.

Propagandist Wang left him frozen in mid-air. 'See?' he said. 'Evidence.'

'Maybe they just want more viewers,' said Li.

Wang smiled thinly. The good times were making everyone lazy. It was a good thing he was here to keep them on track. 'Please,' he said, 'the businessmen own the channels. The government owns the businessmen. Their system is very simple. Don't be fooled by appearances. All of them are one. These telepaths represent your number one priority. Drop your little hobbies and find them.'

'I thought the anti-Party campaign was my number one priority,' said Li.

'That's also your number one priority,' said Wang, 'the Governor will explain to you why.' The Governor looked at him, appalled, a world of hurt in his eyes. He was used to betrayal, but every stab wound was still fresh agony.

'Well, Propagandist Wang is a very fine fellow,' said the Governor, 'so are you, Li, of course. I admire you greatly. Wang can be a little rough at times, but he always has our best interests at heart, assuming he has, um, and then there's the general law and order situation, and intelligence reports. Let's not forget intelligence reports. You need to study those very carefully, along with the Six Precepts of Harmonious Co-Existence, and honestly, Li, telepaths? How can you not be afraid of telepaths? We have no defence against them.'

Governor Wen was terrified of telepaths. He lived in fear that they would peer inside his brain and discover disloyalty to the Young Prince. His transfer to Nagaland as Lesser People's Liaison Officer would be practically instantaneous.

'Not that I mind being defenceless, if it's necessary,' said the Governor. 'Personally, I would lay down my life for the Party. It's the way I was raised, in a village, where we shared bathrooms, and sometimes did it in the fields when it was urgent. But I worry about my colleagues. This could make them nervous and jumpy. Beijing doesn't like it when they get nervous and jumpy. They seem a little crabby already. Please, Li, for their sake, do something about these telepaths. The Cyber Crimes Department says that quite a few have already slipped in. According to them, some are approaching Raj Bhavan, looking for reading material.'

'Is that a fact?' said Li, thoughtfully.

'You'll start investigating, won't you?' said the Governor, 'I would be so relieved. You're so good at it. Isn't he, Wang?'

'He's a prince,' said Wang. He looked at Li. 'So,' he asked, 'are you going to take action on this personal request that the Governor of the province has just made to you?'

'Of course,' said Li.

As soon as he was outside, he called Sexy Chen. 'Now that you're good friends with Crazy Wu, I have a job for you,' he said, ignoring his cries of protest. 'Track those boys. Get their A-cards. I've already given you one. I want to know what they're doing and whom they're meeting. I want to know where they are, every minute of the day. I want to know who gives them money and what they do with it. I want to know everything. And while you're at it, keep an eye on Wu.'

'You think he's the one who did it?' asked Sexy Chen eagerly. 'How did you figure it out? Have you found proof that he's guilty?'

'Everyone's guilty,' said Li.

20

'Is the specimen not satisfactory?'

Sanjeev Verma and his partner Agarwal were in Bagbazaar, peering anxiously down the narrowest, darkest lane that either of them had ever seen. The open sewer babbled like a brook. There were things swimming in it. The rickshaw-wallah had refused to go any further. The crumbling, unwashed buildings on either side were close enough for young lovers to kiss across the balconies, through tangled electric wires. On one of the balconies, an old man sat in a rickety chair, reading *The Statesman* and mumbling to himself. 'Sillyfuckers!' he shouted, suddenly, and subsided. The news was not to his liking.

'How can there be a sweet shop in here?' asked Agarwal, trying not to gag on the stench. 'What type of sweets must they be serving?'

He was fond of sweets, and often advised his barber to work hard and improve his position so that he could afford cashew barfis. He liked encouraging people to be all they could be. He was used to buying sweets from places near his ancestral seat of business on Vivekananda Road, places where the air was cool and the agarbattis fragrant, and everything was fresh except the samosas.

'Just don't buy any,' muttered Verma, who knew his partner well. He hitched up his pants and waded in, not looking down, hoping that it was just water that he felt flowing over his feet.

They were searching for Poltu-da's Wildlife Supply, and had been informed that it was down this lane, right next to Mahesh Chandra Sen's Genuine Brother Ganesh Chandra Sen, a sweet shop rated highly by experts. Their ledigeni was supposed to be a work of art. The sweet itself had been created and named in honour of Lady Canning, the wife of the viceroy just after the mutiny, whose husband had been so touched by this gesture that he had ruled the smouldering country with a very gentle hand, and shown unprecedented solicitude for the natives. 'Darling,' Lady Canning had said, 'look what the dear little sweetmonger just made for me!' 'By Jove!' Lord Canning had replied. 'It looks like these people are all right after all!' His subsequent acts of kindness had earned him the nickname Clemency Canning, bestowed upon him with an intent to wound by those elements of British society who advocated a sterner line with the wogs.

Nearly two hundred years later, another occupant of Raj Bhavan had set in motion a chain of events that had led them here, to this festering cesspool, in search of Poltu-da. Discovered in Bijli Bose's home after her escape from the Pandit Batra Institute for the Criminally Insane, the mercurial and magnetic Pishi had suggested that they present Governor Wen with a tiger penis, as revealed to Agarwal by a shaken Verma, the consumption of which would put lead in his pencil, enabling him to more aggressively pursue peace with the Politburo. Peace was vital to their prosperity. Initially they had hoped that 'tiger penis' was some sort of metaphor or code, but it had turned out that this was not the case.

They stepped gingerly down the lane, the slime slipping under their shoes, and soon crossed Ganesh Chandra Sen's sweet shop, where several flies and a single sandesh were trapped in a dusty glass case. Having carefully assessed supply and demand, Mr Sen made small quantities of sweets, which usually sold out by lunchtime. He spent the rest of the day recovering from his labours. He was currently asleep in a chair with a towel over his face.

A tiny board said 'Poltu-da's Wildlife Supply' just above a narrow door, next to a grimy wall with 'THE PARTY KEEPS 90%' scrawled across it. They trudged up the narrow staircase, trying not to touch the banister. Some of Poltu-da's wildlife was roaming free, and skittering up and down the staircase, invisible in the dark, revealed only by the glow of little red eyes, and the chittering of high little voices.

The reception was tiny. A little boy sat asleep in a chair, his feet up on a small table. A pre-war calendar adorned the wall, with a picture of Dal Lake (which was now toxic). Agarwal cleared his throat. The little boy woke up and was instantly alert.

'Did you bring the stuff?' he asked.

'We've not come to give stuff, we've come to take stuff,' said Agarwal. The little boy considered this.

'What kind of stuff?' he asked cautiously. He was front boy for a variety of enterprises. Their owners lived in a labyrinth of tiny rooms behind him. He provided a bouquet of services, including hospitality, dispatch, catering, office maintenance, massage, and sanitation.

'The usual stuff,' said Agarwal. 'The stuff the others get.'

He was no stranger to this kind of deal. When it came to number-two business, he preferred conducting it personally, since cash was usually involved, but he was always very careful not to incriminate himself.

'Does the stuff wear sarees?' asked the little boy.

'No.'

'Can you smoke the stuff?'

'No.'

'Does the stuff kill your enemies without leaving a trace?'

'No.'

'Does the stuff run on batteries?'

This was likely to go on for a while, Verma could see. It was a Calcutta thing. They lived in a world where time had no meaning. He pushed Agarwal aside. 'We've come here because an ex-CM said this Poltu character could supply us with the noonoo of a tiger, preferably Royal Bengal. It's for a high-class person. If you have it, tell us, otherwise we'll try some other shop.'

'POLTU-DA!' yelled the little boy, 'TWO ANIMAL CUSTOMERS HAVE COME!'

'Please follow me,' said a soft voice with a hint of tuberculosis. Poltu-da had materialized behind them. He was a small man of early middle age, dressed in khaki shorts and a Manchester United jersey. He had a cruel mouth, improbably large hands, and an air of extreme secrecy.

'I keep the merchandise on the roof,' he whispered. 'The sunlight helps them grow.'

It was getting late, and the light was fading on the terrace, which was littered with battered, empty cages big and small, their shapes indistinct in the evening gloom. They followed Poltu-da through the debris to the rear of the terrace, which was modestly illuminated by a single light bulb hanging from a washing line. The first thing they saw was a cage full of rats. The rats climbed over each other in their excitement, hoping they had brought food. Agarwal eyed them with interest. He had no idea there was a market for rats. He had never tracked their price trend.

'People buy rats?' he asked.

'Keep your voice down,' said Poltu-da, 'those are Swiss rats. If the matter becomes public, everyone will come.'

'They don't look very different from Calcutta rats,' said Agarwal.

Poltu-da almost burst out laughing, but he stopped himself just in time.

'Those are just infants,' said Poltu-da. 'Fully grown, they're three to four times the size of local rats, and they shed their baby coats and grow fur as white as the snow-covered Alps. They are much in demand. A leading business family has several. Of course, they take a long time to grow, and the conditions have to be right. Sometimes the transformation is not exact.'

Right next to the Swiss rats was a battered aquarium filled with murky water. Poltu-da noted their interest.

'Invisible fish. From the sea, near Karwar Naval Base. Radiation has caused them to mutate in such a way that human eyesight cannot detect them. Just throw in a handful of puffed rice every day, a few chopped vegetables once a week. Avoid getting your fingers in the water. One of our most popular items. Maintenance cost very low.'

'We don't want Swiss rats or invisible fish,' said Verma, 'we've come here for a tiger.'

'Shhh!' said Poltu-da. 'Don't mention the name. If any of my regular customers find out, I'll have to leave the city. "You had a genuine tiger in stock, Poltu," they will say, as their servants bugger me with a large bamboo, "and you didn't even tell us?" After that they will probably feed me to the animals that I myself have supplied. In this way, the circle of life will be complete, but I will not enjoy it.'

'Look, boss,' said Verma, 'I didn't come all the way from Delhi for someone to fuck me with fekloos. Do you have the goods or not?'

Poltu-da tottered back against a cage, recoiling from all the rudeness. He was the son and grandson of butchers. His great grandfather had played an important role in the Great Calcutta Killings of 1946. More recently, as the population of animals had declined, he had been forced to think out of the box. He was now trading animals wholesale, rather than in bits and pieces. It was much more genteel. The brutishness of this client disturbed him.

'Please don't speak to me in such a fashion,' said Poltu-da, 'my grandpa would have chopped you up with his chopper, but I'm trying not to be like that. If Pishi says I can make the necessary arrangements, then naturally I will keep her word.'

'Let's see the tiger!' said Agarwal. He smiled encouragingly at Poltu-da. He could see some potential in cultivating this man. Many of his friends were crazy about animals. A pet animal was a bigger status symbol than a Rolls-Royce these days. It was a high margin business. This fellow seemed to know the market. Moreover, he was a talented salesman. If he could sell rats, he could sell anything. It was overconfidence on this very score that was just about to bring Poltu-da very close to death at the hands of Verma.

'Certainly, certainly,' said Poltu-da, 'come see the beauty!'

At the end of the terrace was a huge cage covered in tarpaulin. Poltu-da whipped off the tarpaulin with a flourish to reveal a large yellow Sambhalpur cat who had recently had black stripes painted on him. There were dark smudges on the newspaper lining his cage. The cat poked its nose through the bars, sniffing hopefully, whiskers twitching. He seemed like a nice enough creature. Agarwal would have felt sorry for him if he hadn't been so horrified.

'That's a cat!' he said, weakly.

'Of course,' said Poltu-da. 'Tigers *are* cats. It's good that you've been studying the subject. That way, you won't be cheated.'

Verma and Agarwal looked at each other, speechless. Verma briefly considered beating Poltu-da to death, but gave it up as pointless. He could feel a vast hopelessness overcoming him. This happened to him often in Calcutta.

'Even backdoor deals don't happen properly in this city,' he said, sadly. 'Who are we supplying for? The Governor. The biggest Chinese officer in the city. Who are we coming from? A former leader, whose name once curdled milk through the length and breadth of Bengal. Even with such bhao, are we able to get anything? Even after paying money? No, we cannot. This is the mystery of Calcutta.'

Poltu-da was puzzled. 'Is the specimen not satisfactory?'

Verma grabbed him by the scruff of his neck and dragged him close to the cage. 'Does that look like a tiger to you?'

'Well, I've never actually seen one,' said Poltu-da, trying not to suffocate, 'have you? Video can be very deceptive.'

'It's a cat with black paint on it. What we need is the penis of a genuine tiger. High-class Chinese eat them. Don't ask me why.'

'Where on earth would I get a genuine tiger from?' said Poltu-da, appalled. 'Are you out of your mind or what? No one's seen one in twenty years.'

Verma looked at the cat thoughtfully. The cat sneezed. He came to a decision. 'Who's to tell what a tiger's dick actually used to look like?' he said. 'Maybe it wasn't striped. Chalo, give us this piece. Give some discount-shiscount. We'll put it in a nice box. Perhaps no one will notice.'

Poltu-da beamed and started rummaging around happily for his thumbprint reader. He kept it in a box with some extra thumbs, which he used for his duplicate bank accounts.

'Does this mean I won't be able to have children?' said a voice, a little hoarsely. It was the cat. It was sitting there looking at them pathetically.

Agarwal and Verma looked at Poltu-da who looked back at them guiltily. 'I had no idea it could do that,' he said.

'How can you say that?' asked the cat. 'I read the newspaper to you every morning!'

'He's very fluent in Bengali,' said Poltu-da, 'not so good in other languages.'

'If you take away my wee wee, I won't have any babies,' said the cat. 'Then I'll be the only one of my kind. You don't want to do that, do you?'

He arched his back and struck a graceful pose, his chin on the floor of his cage, looking up at them pitifully. They felt themselves wilt under his gaze.

'We can't remove its penis,' said Verma, aghast. 'It's talking!'

'It grows back!' said Poltu-da. 'I've conducted experiments!'

'Why don't you grow your own back!' hissed the cat, trying to slash at him through the bars of his cage

Agarwal put a hand on Poltu-da's shoulder. Despite being a strict vegetarian, he condoned and sometimes even facilitated a wide variety of non-vegetarian activities, but he drew the line at the consumption of sentient beings.

'Mister Poltu, you are a man of parts,' he said. 'I am constantly looking for bright fellows like you. But I am afraid we will have to decline this offer. We will explain everything to Pishi. No one will blame you.'

'You can go blame your mother, you ignorant dick thief!' said the cat, who was rapidly growing in confidence. They could hear him cursing as they walked away.

'Man, that cat would be great at parties,' said Verma, as they negotiated the staircase.

'I think the mistake we're making is we're forgetting our roots,' said Agarwal.

'Does this mean we have to go to the villages?' said Verma. 'My roots are near Chhatarpur. Yours must be some crappy hellhole in the deserts of Rajasthan. They're still radioactive, by the way, because some of the tactical missiles weren't as tactical as they thought they would be.'

'Not necessarily,' said Agarwal. 'What is it we are doing? Trying to find a remedy for a Chinese person. So far, we have pursued Chinese remedies. But ultimately, he is a human being, no? Except for bank balance, we are all the same. The true answer lies in our rich cultural traditions. When it comes to such matters, who has greater skill than the tantric worshippers of the Goddess Kali? Their control over human flesh is unparalleled.'

'So where are we going now?' asked Verma.

'To meet the greatest worshipper of Goddess Kali in Calcutta,' said Agarwal, 'Amalendu Lahiri, General Secretary of the New Thug Society.'

21

*'In our family,
we're more the thinking type.'*

'Cook me some of those birds that I see hopping about the lawns,' said Governor Wen, hoping this would cheer him up. They looked like their bones would be crunchy. He adjusted his aluminium helmet, which had slipped a little. Crazy Wu had built it for him, to protect him against telepaths. It bore a strong resemblance to a bucket, but the Governor was so happy to be safe that no one had had the heart to tell him.

'I'll just go get my air gun,' said Ganguly.

'Don't forget the orange sauce!' Governor Wen called after him. He was touched by his loyalty. Ganguly was the one person he could depend on. Governor Wen was in need of comfort. The quarterly economic data was dreadful, despite extensive massaging, and the Young Prince would be highly displeased.

'Nothing has improved!' he had wailed at the Finance Minister.

The Finance Minister had remained well-bred and tranquil, as befitted a graduate of Presidency College and Harvard, with a house in Jhowtolla Lane.

'This is strictly speaking not true,' he had said.

'Something did improve?' Governor Wen had asked, hopefully.

'Certainly,' his Finance Minister had said, 'our accuracy at estimating the deficit has improved by over 22 per cent. The previous minister was hugely inaccurate in this respect. He has tried to criticize me about this at various public fora, but my analysis has silenced him.'

Ganguly came back with Governor Wen's tea. He had reduced the dosage of the tranquilizers. Docility was one thing, but Governor Wen's inertness was beginning to worry him. He could sense a storm brewing in the Protectorate. Just as he was about to make a big score, and secure his retirement nest egg. It made him uneasy. All his life he had spread his income, taking small amounts of milk from a wide-ranging herd of cows. 'Keep and eat,' an ex-boss had once advised him, 'don't eat everything.' He needed Governor Wen to be at least reasonably alert, so that he could sign things, and appear marginally sentient when he was conferencing with Beijing. The quality of management in Beijing had declined over the years, but they were bound to notice if their potentate turned into a vegetable.

'Have a few sips, Your Excellency,' said Ganguly, 'you'll feel much better.'

Governor Wen took a sip and felt his spirits rise. As he looked at Ganguly, his eyes misted over. 'You take such good care of me,' he said.

'Your Excellency is too kind,' said Ganguly. 'Has Your Excellency had a chance to review the report on Junglemahal?'

Governor Wen felt his spirits dip again. He quickly took another sip.

'What's to review?' he asked. 'They want more guns, as usual. Why are we providing large quantities of arms and ammunition to foreigners, when so many Chinese are still unarmed? It seems unfair. Not that I'm totally against arming foreigners. I would happily give you a gun, my dear Ganguly. Your case is completely different. Is there a particular model I could get you? I could talk to General

Zhou. We can get you anything, so long as it's not Japanese.'

'In our family, we're more the thinking type,' said Ganguly.

He was glad the economic review had missed the inflationary trend in fish prices. The Governor himself would have no idea, of course, since he never bought any. He had never poked one in the belly to check the consistency of its flesh. He had never lifted open a gill flap to see the colour within. He had never tried to judge whether the quantity of fish egg nestling in its bowels was sufficient. He had never rushed home, his filthy nylon bag dripping foul water on feet, footboards, and pavement, to make sure he could present his fish live and thrashing in the kitchen. No, he would remain oblivious to fish until almost the very end, and his fate would be richly deserved.

'Don't worry, Your Excellency, I'll do the needful,' he said, bowing deeply and backing out of the room.

22

*'Li-sahib is a very soft person,
that's why he's not shooting you.'*

'You're in the jungle again, aren't you?' said Gao Yu. She was applying make-up as she spoke. He wished she wouldn't. Why would she need it? He remembered her in Beihei Park snuggled against him, clutching his arm, her cheeks glowing pink and the wind blowing through her hair. Had she not been happy? He could have sworn she was happy. How could he have missed the clues?

'How can you tell?' asked Li. Phoni-babu was peering over his shoulder as they walked towards the Maoist camp. He had no concept of personal space.

'By the expression on your face,' said Gao Yu. 'You were never much fun on holidays. Do you have creepy-crawlies in your shoes?' The thought seemed to please her.

'I do,' said Li, 'but I have to meet the Maoists again. One of the children in my case seems to have joined them.'

'Wow! The famous jungle fighters! Are they handsome? Do they wear shirts?' Gao Yu had always been supremely disinterested in his cases. It was because she wanted him for his body, she had explained.

'Small and malnourished, mostly, like most people in this country,' said Li.

'How can that be? They defeated the might of the Nation Formerly Known As India. The Indians used to be powerful. They took out Nanjing. Are you sure they're real? Maybe they're actors pretending to be Maoists.'

Li could have kissed her, but it seemed odd to shower affection on a screen. 'That's a great question,' he said.

Gao Yu beamed. She held up her arm. She was wearing a yellow silk kimono adorned with a pink dragon, dancing. The sleeve fell back to reveal a diamond bracelet. 'Look what I scored!' she said. 'Worth four-five million, easy. Now it doesn't matter if he leaves me.' She giggled. 'I'll be a leftover woman. Only with lots of money. I'll have Chanel toilet paper and a golden toilet seat. I'll drink Red Pagoda at the Full Moon Lounge, dressed in Issey Miyake. I'll be free to pick and choose. I'm going to pick a man who farts less.'

Li congratulated her. She had never been an easy woman to live with, but she deserved much better than a tuhao from the bogs. He told her this. It did not please her as much as he had thought it would.

'There are all kinds of losers out here,' she said, 'it's not easy. You've got more scope over there. You could try hooking up with the rebel chicks. You might get lucky. They must be desperate, out there in the jungle.'

'I'm just entering the Maoist camp,' he said, 'it looks like they're having some kind of painting competition.'

'Take away their paintbrushes,' said Gao Yu, helpfully. 'They'll tell you everything.' She gave him the finger and vanished.

The guards waved them through. Either they recognized them from the last visit, or security standards were hitting rock bottom. One of them was eyeing a nearby creeper and chewing a pencil thoughtfully. He was holding a sketchpad. They walked past a row of armoured personnel carriers and a mobile rocket launcher. Phoni-babu hissed through his teeth. 'Saala!' he said. 'It seems the junglees have become very modern these days!' The camp appeared to be empty except for the guards. They reached a clearing in front of Debu-da's tent, where they discovered the massed might of the regiment, sprawled on the ground in a variety of poses, drawing pictures. 'ANNUAL SOURIN BOSE MEMORIAL SIT-AND-DRAW COMPETITION' said a banner draped over the perimeter fence.

'It's a Bengali tradition,' said Debu-da, looking natty in his jungle fatigues and a beret. 'Plus it encourages the boys to explore their artistic side. At this stage of the revolution, they need soft skills.'

'What stage of the revolution are we at, exactly?' asked Li. He was curious. Back home there was a lot of debate on this subject.

Debu-da smiled. 'Opinions differ,' he said. 'Some of us feel we're at the let-us-get-on-with-our-work-and-we-won't-blow-you-up stage, as defined by Comrade KS. That's when we consolidate our gains and concentrate on uplifting the local people, who've been waiting for a long time. Others have acquired a taste for elimination, and feel we haven't eliminated enough capitalists yet. They want to liberate Hyderabad, because it's our spiritual centre, and Patna, because the Bihari boys want it. Some of them want to take Bhopal, so they can launch an attack on Delhi in the next phase. I'm no military genius, but it sounds pretty stupid. In all our history, who's ever conquered Delhi from Bhopal?'

Inspector Li stepped gingerly amongst the artists. What did revolutionary armies draw? How did they express themselves through art? Mindful of Gao Yu's advice, he stopped in front of one of the girls. She was doe-eyed and full-lipped. He bent down to look at her drawing. It was a blood-spattered earthen pitcher filled with milk. As he watched, she added more blood. She looked up. 'It's the blood of Visunuri Deshmukh,' she explained. 'Our sisters used to labour in his fields. When they begged him to let them feed their babies, he would collect their milk in pots, and pour it out on the ground, laughing. We hacked him down in his field one day, and his blood mingled with our milk. We fertilized the ground with his flesh.'

These were new fables for a new society. Not the best stories to put a child to sleep with, but maybe they wanted them to stay awake. He looked back at Phoni-babu, standing on the sidelines. His expression was saintly and encouraging, his lathi held behind his back. He knew when he was outgunned. 'Sir, finish quickly, sir, and then let us talk to Mr Debu,' he said. 'Soon it will be dark. Even flying, it's two hours to Lal Bazaar.'

'Let them draw, come on in,' said Debu, holding up the flap of his tent. They stepped in. 'You never told me one of Barin Mondol's boys had joined you,' said Li, 'you're hiding things from the police.'

'You're not my police,' said Debu, grinning to show he meant no offence. 'So many kids join up, it's hard to keep track. How did you find out?'

'A local hero named Geju is running the boys on the street,' said Li. 'He said one of them joined you here, soon after the murder. That's why I'm back in the jungle. Boy named Toobloo.'

'Very sweet name for a boy,' said Phoni-babu. 'Toobloos have a tendency to be plumpish. My neighbour has a nephew named Toobloo. He can eat like anything.'

'Can I meet the boy, please?' said Li.

'I don't see why not,' said Debu-da, 'he needs to lose his fear of Chinese people.'

'From what I've seen of these boys,' said Li, 'fear of Chinese people is not a problem.' Debu-da stuck his head out of the tent. 'Hey, Toobloo, there's a cop here to see you!' he yelled.

They were joined shortly by a serious little boy in spectacles, dressed in a regulation uniform which was slightly too big for him. Li knew they were small for their age here, but he was still shocked. He had a rifle slung over his shoulder and a sheet of paper in his hand. 'Who ratted me out?' he demanded. 'It was Gonsha, wasn't it? He's a number one gandoo. His brain is slow, but his tongue is quick. Nothing stays in his stomach. You have to beat him up from time to time. He was spoilt by his sisters. They were so happy to get a little brother, they treated him like the son of Nawab Khanja Khan. I told the others we should kick him out. Big mouth, empty stomach.'

'Well, you're out of it now, aren't you?' said Li.

'There was nothing left,' said Toobloo, 'What were we going to do without Mister Master? Who was going to take his place? Geju? All he wants is money. He's saving up for a plastic randi. Mister Master never liked him. He said he was the lumpen component of the proletariat. The others were keen to continue, but I saw no future. Debu-da seems like a good person. He's promised to get us all married to local girls. It's time I started a family.'

'Not just yet,' said Debu-da, smiling.

'And what were you doing, exactly?' asked Li.

'Selling, what else? You think Geju-da does charity? In fact, right now he's very upset. Less of us on the streets means less money for him. He was blaming you. "I'm going to squash his balls," he said, "and make him sing like Lata Mangeshkar." Meanwhile Mister Master is dead. Foget about me, what are you doing? Have you arrested the thugs yet?'

'I met their boss,' said Li, 'very fine gentleman.'

'Those are the worst,' said Toobloo. 'They're too lazy to suck blood. They make other people do it for them. Sometimes they have chilli chicken and fried rice at the Calcutta Club. Sometimes they read poetry. Other than that, they do nothing. All their money comes from number-two business. Why did he kill Mister Master? Did you ask, or did you arrive at a settlement?'

There was only so much Phoni-babu could digest. 'Maoist-

Taoist I don't know, you manage your mouth, or things won't be good! Whole life I've upheld the honour of this uniform, you can't insult it just like that! Li-sahib is a very soft person, that's why he's not shooting you.'

'Who let this uncle in, Debu-da?' asked Toobloo. 'Can we give him some treatment? I'll call the others.'

Debu-da folded his hands. 'Please take a seat, dada, I'll ask for a cup of tea. Don't mind the boy. We teach these young boys to be strong. Sometimes they become too strong. Don't mind. We all respect your Inspector very much. He's not just handsome, he's highly intelligent. Possibly honest also.' Phoni-babu subsided, mollified by his charm.

'I don't do settlements,' said Li. 'If Amalendu Lahiri of the Thug Society is the culprit, I'll take him in. I'm just not sure yet. You're a smart boy. You know it's not always that simple. Are you sure it was the thugs? And if they did it, then why?'

The boy's face crumpled. He was a bold little monkey, like most of them. But he was still a child. 'I don't think about it,' he said, 'I don't want to think about it. What's the point? He's gone.'

'Well, there's always revenge,' said Li, 'it's one of the things I'm looking for. Vengeance, love, silence, money. That's why most crimes happen. I just don't know which one's the cause of this crime.'

The little boy wiped his eyes. 'I hope you find out. If you need any help, let me know. Debu-da will give me off.' Debu-da put his arm round the boy's shoulder. 'Of course I will,' he said. 'Come on, Inspector. You've harassed enough children for one day.'

'I'm not the one teaching them to kill people,' said Li, 'but I have to thank you for the book. It was interesting. Felt just like home.' He reached into his jacket and handed back his copy of *Animal Farm*. Debu-da snatched it from him quickly and shoved it under a pile of clothes on his cot. His smile seemed a little forced. 'Why, thank you, inspector! I completely forgot. I thought you would keep it. It's a rare and precious thing. You really are an honest man.'

Before leaving, Li turned to his young suspect, who had abruptly stopped crying. 'What are you going to do now?' asked Li.

'Think,' said Toobloo.

Just as they reached their car, parked on the edge of the jungle, Phoni-babu received a phone call. His mouth fell open as he listened. 'What are you saying, sisterfucker!' he cried. 'How is that even possible? Which mother's son would dare to do such a thing?' The phone dropped from his nerveless fingers. He fell at Inspector Li's feet. He wrapped his arms around his knees. To Li's amazement, there were tears in his eyes.

'Sir, please save us! Please do something!' he said. 'You're a brave officer!'

'Save you from what?' asked Li, trying to pull him back to his feet.

'Maa Kali have mercy on us all! They're destroying the Kalighat Temple!'

'Who is?'

'You, Inspector-sahib, you! Soldiers have come, with tanks. They're blowing up our temple and shooting the priests! How could you do this? We look upon you as our elder brothers. We serve you with maximum loyalty. Big Chen refuses, but every penny of my collection, I share with Sexy!'

'Crying won't help your mother. Get off your feet and get in the car,' said Li. 'I'm dropping you off at the station on the way.'

23

*'All it requires is a systematic approach,
and enough ammunition.'*

Inspector Li watched the Kalighat Temple burn. A black tank with the insignia of the People's Armed Police was parked horizontally across the tram tracks. It fired off a round, obliterating three small shops and a legless beggar, who was unarmed, unless you counted his small tin bowl, which flew up in the air, miraculously intact. One of the soldiers fired from the hip, and hit the bowl, earning a cheer from some of his comrades. Joy was not universal. Some of the others were looking away, their rifles pointed at the ground. General Zhou watched, feet planted wide apart, hands on his hips, smiling.

'What do you think you're doing?' said Inspector Li.

The hysterical crowd pressed against the barricade, maddened by grief. General Zhou gave the sign and his boys opened fire. 'Try not to shoot any children,' he shouted, out of deference to his guest. He liked Inspector Li, even though he was from the Ministry of Internal Security. He could hold his drink, and he knew when to hold his tongue, priceless qualities, both.

'Why are you doing this?' asked Inspector Li.

General Zhou slapped him on the back. He belonged to the whistle-while-you-work school of soldiering. He was fat, cheerful, and thick as a plank. His men loved him to bits.

'First, let me tell you, little brother, this has nothing to do with quotas. It's true we were slightly behind. The Governor's been very busy, and he won't let us use his lawn. He seems a little depressed. We need to keep an eye on the fellow. This has nothing to do with him. This is a patriotic forward movement, to help save the Motherland.'

A wizened old priest emerged from the smoke, clasping a small idol to his breast, followed by an impossibly burdened flower boy, wearing most of his merchandise round his neck. The guns had stopped firing now. The crowd was creeping in, to remove the dead and the dying. Some still stood at the barricades, watching the temple burn, their faces lit by the fire.

'Once the ashes cool, we'll go in and check how many thugs we got,' said General Zhou.

'Thugs?' echoed Inspector Li, hollowly.

'Yes, thugs,' said General Chen, eyeing his troops keenly for signs of battle fatigue. 'I heard about your meeting with Wang. Apparently, he thinks the thugs are no threat. His brain is the size of his penis. Of course they're a threat! They've killed four of us in the last six weeks. That's the problem with you Internal Security people, you spend too much time stuck to computers. The People's Armed Police believes in action. Spend more time on the streets, meet lots of people, shoot them. That's the way to do it.'

'But I thought Propagandist Wang specifically ordered us to focus on the telepaths, who are crossing the border as we speak,' said Inspector Li.

'I don't report to that dog turd,' said General Zhou, frostily, 'I report directly to Beijing. Once I explained the situation, their orders were very precise. There's this ancient cult or brotherhood, I said, who are going around killing Chinese officials with handkerchiefs. I explained how they were deadly secret, and masters of disguise, and worshipped a goddess named Kali. As I had anticipated, the news of a secret religious cult terrified them. They asked for my advice. They know I'm an expert on local conditions.'

General Zhou was a war veteran, and proud of it. He'd seen action during the Ranchi Incident, which had mostly involved retreating from Ranchi. The Maoists had warned them about Indians advancing in overwhelming numbers. The rumours had turned out to be false, but the Maoists had promised to hold the ground for them, and to keep them posted about future threats.

'If the roots are not removed during weeding, the weeds will return when the spring wind blows,' said General Zhou. 'We need simple logic, and an iron hand. The thugs worship Kali. No Kali, no thugs. We've made a list of all Kali temples in the Protectorate. We will destroy each and every one of them. Left with no goddess to pray to, the New Thug Society will wither away, like capitalism. All it requires is a systematic approach, and enough ammunition.'

Inspector Li sat down on a nearby sandbag. 'What did they say about your plan?' he asked.

'Oh, they agreed. Of course, things are different in the Motherland. Society has evolved. No one shoots cult members now. We adjust them instead. But in the New Territories, the old rules still apply. Once the GDP reaches a certain level, more freedom will be allowed. I'm not sure what the required GDP level is exactly, but it will be revealed once we reach it. Until then, we run over them with tanks, as and when required. That's the essence of our philosophy.'

I could do with some adjustment myself, thought Li. Maybe then my head won't hurt so much.

'If we can finish the job in four weeks, all my boys get free holidays in Macau, and luxury flats in Celestial Heights. Celestial Heights! Can you imagine? For a new man, no place is better than the New Territories!'

Inspector Li knew the score. Almost everything boiled down to real estate in the end. He looked curiously at the soldiers. Not all of them were as excited by the prospect of flats as General Zhou. Several were muttering. As he watched, one of them threw down his rifle. The others tried to make him pick it up, but he refused, shaking his head. Finally an officer scooped it up and handed it back to him. He took no further action, and walked away.

Darkness had fallen. The burning temple lit up the night. The crowds were bigger now. The air was filled with the sound of crying, and something else. Young men, whispering to each other. There was more than just mourning in the whispers. A new chapter was about to be written in the history of imperialism with Chinese characteristics.

He felt a hand on his shoulder. He looked up. It was Big Chen. His face was set like stone. 'We need to move, boss,' he said. 'There's been an incident at Bijli Bose's house.'

Li bounced to his feet. 'What do you mean by incident?'

'Assassination attempt. Thug. Been arrested. Also an old man attacked him with a signboard.'

'What, two people tried to murder him at the same time?'

'I don't think he's very popular,' said Big Chen.

'Or one of them wasn't trying to kill him,' said Li. 'Let's go find out.'

They walked back to the car in the gathering dark, as the whispers grew, and the flames flickered over the temple.

24

*'See what sign I'm making now,
you evil old dead body!'*

'Pass the tobacco,' said the thug, smiling a private smile.

Inspector Li lit a cigarette from his own and passed it on. He was in an interrogation room in the heart of Lal Bazaar. Generations of suspects had sweated it out in these rooms, cowering at the sight of chillies. The atmosphere was discouraging. The lights were dim. The air was oppressive. The walls were laced with grime and fear. The contrast with home was striking. Everything in Beijing police stations was shiny and new. The instruments were sharp, and the lighting was fabulous. Money was never a constraint. Here it was different. The government spent very little, and lawmen were expected to live off the land. The public was their primary source of income. Apart from selecting the officers, which was done for a modest fee, the government had little role to play. There was no incentive for capital investment, which was why most of their facilities were horrible. Inspector Li had read about the Black Hole of Calcutta, a case involving the suffocation of white people. In 1857, rebellious natives had put a large number of Britons into a small cell. Not used to being so close to each other, many had expired. Enraged by this atrocity, the British had soundly thrashed the natives, and proceeded to siphon money out of India even faster than before. It all seemed like a perfectly simple misunderstanding to Li. He could imagine the jailors looking down the next morning and shaking their heads in wonder. 'Just one night,' they would have said to each other, 'that's all they had to spend in it. Such weaklings they are. We can beat these people.'

The thug was dressed in an ordinary white shirt and blue jeans. He was in his mid-thirties, with neatly cut hair. He could have been a front office man at Hong Kong Bank. Perhaps he was. The thugs were tricksy, and never visibly thug-like. It was the secret of their success. Their clothes might have changed, but the approach was the same. His complexion was fair, which meant he was most probably upper caste. Inspector Li was yet to figure out what exactly this implied, although he had a hunch that it was far more complex than some people thought. He had met some fat cats from the sweeper caste, and if they were groaning under millennia of oppression, they were hiding it very well.

'Why aren't you afraid?' he asked.

'I take strength from your courage.'

'How much courage can it take to strangle a man in his sleep?' asked Inspector Li, who disliked receiving compliments from murderers.

'It's not such an easy thing,' said the thug, not in the least bit offended. It was a common misconception amongst laymen, one for which he did not blame them. 'It requires courage, skill, and devotion. Above all it requires the touch of the goddess. The goddess has put me on this earth for a purpose. I am the hunter, and you are the prey. If a tiger performs its duty with a deer, will you call it a murderer?'

'His name was Barin Mondol,' said Inspector Li, 'the woman next door was in love with him. He was trying to help the village children learn something so that they could get ahead in life. He liked reading Tolstoy. He worked in a government office and he never took any money from anyone. You crept up on him in the middle of the night and you strangled him like a chicken. That makes you a murderer. You're no tiger. No one's going to put you in a zoo. They're going to put you on a badly constructed wooden stand, and then they're going to put a rope around your neck and hang you, which is the perfect way to go for a little shit like you. Alternatively, you can give us some names and details, instead of all these guidelines from the goddess, and you might just spend the rest of your life in jail, using your courage and skill to prevent your bum from being taken.'

Inspector Li had never believed in the good cop-bad cop system. It was just another way in which Americans complicated simple things. Set them up and knock them down, that was how you did it. Just like his dad used to say. Hard and fast, without warning. Sometimes they went down. Sometimes they swung back wildly, revealing themselves. The trick was to keep them off balance.

'I like you,' said the thug, taking a deep drag on his cigarette and gagging slightly. He had never smoked Long March before. 'I will be leaving soon. You will not see me coming or going. I think you are a gentleman, although you are pretending not to be, so we will leave you for the last.'

'That's very kind of you,' said Inspector Li, reaching across the grubby plastic table to pat him on the back. 'Just before you leave, why don't you tell me about this Japanese-Bengali phrasebook you've been carrying. Planning a holiday in Tokyo are we?'

The thug said nothing. His air of calm superiority was beginning to get to Li. He was an upper-class twit, just like his mentor, Amalendu Lahiri, who talked big and starved his servants. Inspector Li looked at the items laid out on the table. The phrasebook, a huge wad of cash, a yellow silk handkerchief, a Japanese business card, and a small coin. The cash was all local. The amount was astonishing. It was one of the things that had put him in a foul mood. Purity of purpose he could understand, even admire a little. But it looked like they were in it for the money. And there was definitely something fishy going on. All you had to do was smell the man.

'Why Bijli Bose?' he asked.

He had been apprehended while trying to assassinate the venerable elder. The thug was not the only criminal they had picked up. The star of the evening had undoubtedly been a demented sixty-year-old signboard-maker with wild white hair, who had slipped into Bijli Bose's home and attempted to beat him to death with a signboard which said 'Learn English in 60 Days!' 'I never learnt English because of you!' he had roared, leaping into the living room, where Bijli Bose was having a small Scotch and soda. 'In the end I had to make signboards! See what sign I'm making now, you evil old dead body!'

Bijli Bose had evaded his attacker with a surprising burst of speed. The man's rage was a direct consequence of the old man's decree, implemented across Bengal during his disturbingly long rule, that everyone else's children should study only in Bengali in order to properly preserve their innate Bengali-ness, towards the dilution of which imperialist forces were constantly striving. Meanwhile, he had ensured that his own children all went to English medium schools, so that they could infiltrate the enemy from within. He had maintained this policy strictly until he was surgically removed from the chief minister's chair. The chair had in fact fused partially with his backside, something that was not widely publicized at the time.

Along with the agitated signboard maker, the security forces had apprehended the thug, who had also crept into the sitting room around the same time, and had been sitting in an armchair just across from Bijli Bose. He had no doubt been lulling Bijli Bose into a false sense of security, the security chief had said, waiting for the right moment to strike. It was what they did. No one knew how he had got in, which was quite natural, given that he was a thug. The signboard maker had gotten past security by pretending to be a representative of the Better English Company, come to seek blessings from the mummified ex-chief minister. No one had asked him why he was carrying a signboard instead of a leaflet. The thug had been caught because of bad luck, pure and simple. Who could have predicted simultaneous attempts at murder?

But why would they want to kill Bijli Bose? And how was this connected to the death of Barin Mondol? He couldn't see the connection. Unless, of course, there was no connection.

'Why does the New Thug Society want to kill Bijli Bose?'

The thug burst out laughing. He was genuinely amused.

The confidence of criminals in Indian jails never ceased to astonish him. At least in China they felt fear. This man was behaving like a guest at a cocktail party. Inspector Li took deep breaths.

'Why indeed?' said the thug, 'since he can come back from the dead? Clearly, the goddess has no use for him.'

Inspector Li looked at the smiling thug. He stubbed out his cigarette with a certain precision and force. Some things were clear. Others were grey. For example, what was Bijli Bose up to? He knew he'd had meetings with Agarwal and Verma, an unholy two-reed opera from which nothing good was likely to emerge. Inspector Li knew Agarwal to be a man who delighted in the company of large sums of money. Wherever a river of money flowed, he would be there, an ardent devotee, knees knocking in the early morning chill. How would Agarwal use this situation to make money? Their slave mines were in the Chhatisgarh Free Zone, in between the potential combatants. When dragons fought, ducks were roasted, which was why they were trying to stop a war. But even in distress, Agarwal was not the kind of man to miss an opportunity.

'You've been a great help,' said Li, 'you sat there like a film star and refused to answer questions, but I learnt a lot from your pockets. And you're not much of a gentleman if you stink like that. Ask your boss to get you some cologne. Tell him that he'd better stop this racket. Tell him that if I reveal what I know, the good people of Bhobanipur are going to come and burn down his house.'

As he turned to leave, one of the guards caught his eye. He put his finger to the back of the thug's head and looked at Li inquisitively. Inspector Li smiled and put a hand on his shoulder.

'Try keeping this one alive, son,' he said, 'you might learn something that way.'

25

*'Chhooo chhooo chhooo mantar...gili
gili gili...hocus pocus...bhanish!'*

Security had been increased at Bijli Bose's house, so he was safe from thugs, but not from Pishi. She was standing behind his chair, singing.

'No ooman, no cry,' she sang sadly, 'no ooman, no cry.'

'What is she singing?' whispered Li. They were standing near the door, waiting politely for her recital to finish, ignoring the faint hint of desperation in the eyes of Bijli Bose. Li disliked the man. From what he had understood, he had caused a lot of suffering, and never displayed much empathy for his victims. It was only fair that he should suffer a little himself.

'It is a song of Ali the Wanderer,' said Phoni-babu, 'famous Baul singer from last century. He was a lost soul who travelled from village to village, singing such songs and promoting smoking of ganja. Some say he was looking for Netaji Subhas Chandra Bose, a great leader of our freedom struggle, who was misplaced by the Japanese. His songs were very catchy, and subject matter was very different, such as buffaloes who became soldiers, and liberal use of jam, and the shooting of one Sharif. Nowadays, we prefer simple songs, like "Bye Bye Bangkok" and "Hello Memsahib", but few cultured people still remember him. Pishi is very talented and cultured. Historically her behaviour has shown that. Either she was writing, or she was reciting, or she was singing songs.'

Pishi drifted into the adjacent bedroom. 'Probably she is going to paint,' said Phoni-babu.

Now that Bijli Bose was no longer being tortured, Inspector Li stepped forward into the room. 'Good to see you safe, sir,' he said.

'Who says I'm safe?' said Bijli Bose, morosely. 'She hasn't even started reciting her poetry yet. She wrote thirty-seven volumes.' His trembling hand reached for his whisky glass. He was too depressed to pretend that he was a mummy.

'That's something to look forward to then,' said Li, brightly. 'I was curious. What led you to give shelter to a wanted fugitive and known splittist? Since it's you, no one's worried, given how loyal you've always been. But you were never the best of friends, were you? I understand your boys once cracked her skull. She spent ten days in hospital. She may be old, but she's still more active than you. Isn't this a little risky? Supposing she creeps up on you in the middle of the night, looking for revenge?'

'You seem to feel that I could stop her,' said Bijli Bose. 'She just came in through the bathroom window one day and said, "Bijli-da, I'm staying with you." Her actions are devoid of logic. That's why we could never manage her. The Party was built on logic and discipline. We had no guidelines for handling eccentricity. Of course, she was not always like this. She went mad trying to get Bengali bureaucrats to work, something I very wisely avoided trying to do. I am hoping that at some point some other brainwave will strike her, and she will go. Currently she is very upset about the destruction of the Kali Temple. That's why she was consoling herself with the song. She is a great devotee. During her rule, all portraits of Marx were replaced with portraits of the Mother. Luckily she has no followers now, otherwise the matter could become complicated. But the potential for unrest exists. The boys used to love her. If they see her again, they could get excited. It's why I'm trying to keep her in the house.'

'Good luck with that,' said Li, grabbing Phoni-babu's arm. Phoni-babu was about to slip off into the bedroom, to see what Pishi was up to. He was clearly fascinated, perhaps even a little bit in love. 'Mother! Destruction of Mother!' they heard her cry. 'Revenge is required on Chinese! But I am ooweek!' Followed by the sound of weeping.

'So, no one noticed the thug coming in?' asked Li. 'You have a large staff here, protecting you.'

'It's their nature. They come and go. They mingle.'

'Did he mingle with you? Apparently he was caught in the living room, sitting in an armchair. Almost as if you were having a meeting.'

'I did not realize he was a thug,' said Bijli Bose. 'The victims never do. He said he was a reporter, come to do a story on the golden era of Bengal. Also, he wanted to read me his novel. All of them have novels, except for the ones who write poems. That's the fundamental problem with Bengal. Too much poetry. Poetry obscures. I prefer prose.'

'Well, lucky for you the man with the signboard chose that very moment to try and beat your brains out,' said Li. 'That's what alerted the guards.'

Pishi drifted back into the room, making graceful hand movements. She noticed Li for the first time. She ignored Phoni-babu, who was gazing at her adoringly. 'Who is dis?' she demanded.

'He's an officer protecting me from the thugs,' said Bijli Bose.

'You're the biggest thug, Bijli-da,' she said, morosely. 'Who will protect them from you?'

She bent down to peer at Li's face. Li smiled back at her. He liked a woman with spirit. She looked into his eyes, searching. She seemed pleased. 'You are honest policeman!' she said, astonished,

'Towards end of my time, I sarched and sarched, thinking, hwer are you? But it waj phelyur. I had remoobhed all of dem. I should habh supported them more. Meanwhile, gorment babus were making everything bhanish! True magicians, better dan P. C. Shorcar. How could I do development? Money going for school, bephor it riches, bhanish! Money going for flood rilif, but bephor it riches, bhanish! Chhooo chhooo chhooo mantar...gili gili...hocus pocus...bhanish! But I am still here. I am still libhing. I will not let Bengal become nonsense place like India, becoj of Competent Authority. He haj taken everything! But here, I will not allow. I am gonodebota—goddess of da pipool!'

'Pipool?' asked Li.

'Common pipool!' explained Pishi. 'You are good man! You do your job, I am supporting you. If you phace any poblem, come back soon, I ooweel help you. But be carephool of Mowists—dey are ebhrywheyar. And beware of dis Bijli-da. Dese gentry fellow cannot be trusted. Olways doing number-two bijness. '

'I'll keep that in mind,' said Li. Could it have been her? She was a force of nature. Through sheer force of will, she had subjugated one of the most Machiavellian minds of the twentieth century. Had she engineered the elimination of Barin Mondol as a suspected Maoist? Li hated it when crazy people got involved in his cases. You could never predict what they were going to do next. On the other hand, there was never any harm in asking.

'What are your future plans, old mother?' he asked.

She flashed him a smile, and in that moment Li realized why so many had once followed her. She bent down and whispered in his ear. 'I ham oowaiting phor da right moment,' she said. 'Storm is coming. Can you not pheel it? Can you not hear it?' She listened for a moment and smiled, satisfied. 'Bhery soon! Bhery soon!' She drifted off, taking tiny little dance steps, clipping Bijli Bose lightly on the side of the head as she passed.

Big Chen called. His face was grim. 'Geju's here,' he said, 'the one who manages the boys. Looking for a fight. He brought his drone. Its language is filthy.'

'Don't knock him out,' said Li, who knew Big Chen well. His views in such matters were simple and direct. 'I need to ask him some questions. Things are moving fast.'

Li excused himself and left, dragging Phoni-babu, who was inclined to linger.

'What a woman!' said Phoni-babu, peering back at the bedroom door. 'Because of her, even in this dark time there is still hope!'

26

*'All I am doing is serving you loyally,
without ever asking for return.'*

They saw faint wisps of smoke as they flew over the city, people were filling the streets. Black armoured cars of the People's Armed Police dotted the landscape, but the cars were few, and the people were many. Somewhere in the distance, they heard the dull thump of a mortar. As they got out in front of the station, they were almost knocked over by a Chinese vendor, hurrying off with his tin trunk on his head. He did not stop to apologize. He was followed by others. They had been selling prawn wafers and meat pies in the little lane behind Lal Bazaar since 1853, but some sixth sense was telling them that their time was up. Old China was leaving. The rest was up to New China. Big Chen opened his mouth to speak, but Inspector Li was already striding into the building. He had a case to wrap up.

Geju-da had come dressed for the occasion, in a crisp white linen shirt over his blue-checked lungi. His drone hovered over his left shoulder, small, jet-black and menacing.

'Acchha, Inspector-sahib, so finally you've come. Good you could find the time. Your hotka assistant is not cooperating, just standing there like a cut soldier. He pretends as if he doesn't understand anything. But I understand everything. You think I'm a goatfucker? I won't accept this. It won't be good, I'm telling you. Geju doesn't fear anyone.'

'What's your problem?' asked Li.

'Poblem? I'll tell you the poblem. You're hitting me in my stomach, that's the poblem. You hit my stomach, I won't let you go!'

'Won't let you go, gandoo!' echoed the drone, firing a laser bolt at the ceiling. It sliced through the blade of a ceiling fan, leaving it dangling limply.

'I haven't hit you in the stomach yet,' said Li, 'but I can if you want me to.'

'Jokes? You're making jokes, sillyfucker? I'll show you jokes!'

Big Chen made a move towards him. Li waved him back. Even Phoni-babu was appalled. 'Chhee chhee, Geju, is this any way to talk?' he said. 'What will people think? Try to be cultured.' Since his meeting with Pishi, he was acutely conscious of culture.

'Oye, who asked you to speak? Big talk in small mouth! Go beat up a rickshaw-wallah. Don't give me dialogue, I'll change your face-cutting.'

Phoni-babu turned to Li, hands raised in supplication. He was on the verge of tears. 'Sir, where is the dignity?' he wailed. 'Thirty years I have honoured this uniform. Naturally between goonda-class and police people some amount of adjustment is required. But in front of you he is speaking like this? How much more must I suffer? All I am doing is serving you loyally, without ever asking for any return.'

'You still haven't told me your problem,' said Li. He was extremely calm. This was a bad sign. Big Chen loosened his holster.

'Stop messing with my boys! It's not going to be good, I'm telling you. My boys are my income. I support them, they support me. Anybody interferes, dead bodies will drop. You don't know who I am. I started as a wagon-breaker, moved on to bladder business, now look at me today! Four-four cars in the garage! You think it happened just like that? All these people I'm feeding. Where would they be without me? All the time I'm supporting society. None of you high-class people do anything, only I am there. Tomorrow if there's an election, do you think they'll vote for you?'

'Long live Geju!' said the drone, 'Geju live long!'

The nerve of Bengali goons never ceased to amaze him. From funerals to weddings to flag hoistings, there was no time or place where they feared policemen. Not even inside police stations. The man was acting as if he owned the place.

'They're witnesses in my case,' said Li, 'it's part of my job.'

'Saala! You're showing me job? You think I'm a fool?'

The drone began to crackle again, warming up its laser. 'Who says that?' it demanded. 'Who? Who?'

'Leave my boys alone, I'm telling you,' said Geju. 'You're an agent of Debu Maoist, don't think I don't know. You're all in it together, sucking the blood of the people! You've been eating their brains, meeting my boys and doing gujguj-phusphus. One by one, they're leaving. Just now Toobloo joined them. Feeding them, clothing them, all this training I gave, what, so that just like that they can walk away? Don't try to be clever with me. Result will not be good. You like the little boys so much, one-two bodies I can send you. Then we can see.'

'Why don't you go and fuck yourself?' said Li.

'Haramjada!' roared Geju-da, lunging for him. 'Shoot the drone' said Li. Big Chen drew fast and fired from the hip. The drone exploded spectacularly. Li took Geju-da down with a single clean uppercut to the jaw. The goon dropped like a stone, settling into a boneless heap on the floor, covered in shards of drone.

Li rubbed his knuckles. Thanks to his father, he was a boxer in a land of kung-fu.

'Do you think he did it?' asked Big Chen. 'Maybe he and the teacher had a fight over the boys? Then he killed him and made it look like the thugs?'

'Lock him up and we'll see,' said Li.

His phone rang. It was Sexy Chen. He looked guilty.

'It's probably not your fault,' said Li.

'You asked me to track those two boys,' he said.

'Where are they?' asked Li.

'That's the thing. We don't know,' said Sexy Chen, 'I don't see how it's possible, but they've disappeared off the grid.'

'Sounds like a job for Crazy Wu,' said Li. 'Funny how he keeps popping up, isn't it? Join me in the basement.'

'How can they just go off the grid like that?' asked Big Chen. 'We took their A-cards.'

'Maybe they didn't,' said Li.

27

*'Don't let him touch my feet just now,
there's money on them.'*

As Calcutta went up in flames, a small evening celebration was going on at the home of Bijli Bose. He raised his glass in a toast.

'To the Proletariat!' said Bijli Bose.

'To the Proletariat!' said Propagandist Wang.

They had much to thank the proletariat for. Rioting had started in the streets. Buses were burning. The systematic and clandestine removal of all fish from Calcutta, as suggested by Bijli Bose, had pushed them over the edge. His own suggestion of a Xinjiang-style programme against Kali temples had helped. It looked like war would be averted. There would be some temporary pain, but it would all be for the betterment of both their people.

'Your contribution was invaluable, Mr Bose,' he said, 'you not only thought of the idea, you chose the right people for the job. To conduct a secret operation in Calcutta markets, who better than the thugs? All due to your guanxi with their leader.'

'All of us know each other in Bengal,' said Bijli Bose modestly. 'Lahiri and I are both members of the Calcutta Club. Bit obsessed with temples, but otherwise a sound fellow. My paternal cousin sister married his maternal uncle-brother.'

'They are masters of deceit, those thugs,' said Wang, 'much

better than those inferior Japanese ninjas. One of them was arrested yesterday, by the way. He was pretending to be a momo seller in front of the LIC building on Chittaranjan Avenue. His costume was perfect but his stove gave him away. It had robot arms and a dish antenna, and it kept giving passers-by tips on nutrition. In the evenings, he was making pathetic attempts in local markets to locate fish. Apparently, this was why he had come, although he had misplaced his master, who was a trader of fish. We gave him a small packet of prawns and put him on a flight to Tokyo.'

'Your bit about the FARS virus was a masterstroke,' said Bijli Bose. 'It added to the panic and the resentment. For maximum impact, you should go on TV in the evening and deny it. Things have worked out well. It looks like you'll be back in Beijing soon. Have you found yourself a suitable position?'

'Why go just yet?' said Wang. 'Perhaps I could contribute to bringing peace to the province, and go back a hero.' This could easily be achieved by releasing some of the fish back in the market. He had not shared this part of the plan with Bijli Bose. He wanted to act swiftly and make sure he got all the credit. All he had to do was find out *where* Bijli Bose was keeping the fish.

'Your mind never stops working.'

'Your wisdom inspires me.'

'You know, it's true what Nehru said.'

'You mean, it's true what imperialist stooge Nehru said,' corrected Propagandist Wang, gently.

Bijli Bose raised his glass again. 'It's true what imperialist stooge Nehru said. Hindi-Chini Bhai Bhai!'

They clinked glasses and drank to that.

A brick smashed through the window, landing on the carpet near their feet, followed by the sound of an explosion outside. Two servants in white appeared instantly, and briskly brushed up the glass. Bijli Bose frowned slightly. His armchair drifted to the right, away from the window. The small table with the glass followed.

Verma burst into the room, followed by Agarwal. They were dishevelled and bore signs of recent manhandling.

'The public appears to be angry,' said Bijli Bose.

'Angry?' said Verma. 'They're out of their fucking minds! These Bengalis pretend to be quiet and sophisticated, wearing spectacles and not going to the gym, but they're a bunch of lunatics. I've been checking their history. Twice they've trashed the Eden Gardens. Every week they burn buses. Not to mention the freedom struggle. It's like Kashmir out there. I saw some local boys spray a tank with chilli powder. The mounted police are useless because the horses are terrified. And which genius issued the prawn crackers to the troops? I saw a crowd pounce on a platoon and strip them down to their underwear. I saw men on the street selling pictures of fish. I saw a column of vegetarians leaving the city, clinging to their meager belongings, looking back sadly. I saw a little old lady smash the window of a pet shop, and stagger off with an aquarium. The little fish swam about in it hopelessly.'

Silence fell over the room, punctuated by the occasional homemade bomb. Propagandist Wang excused himself and left. Propaganda played a key role in times of crisis. He had further work to do involving the FARS virus.

Agarwal nudged Verma. He was trying to teach him manners. It was an uphill task, but he refused to give in. Verma cleared his throat. 'We want to express our gratitude, Bijli-uncle,' he said, 'for all the benefits you have given us. We wanted massive gadar in Calcutta, and thanks to you, massive gadar has been created. Your idea of removing all the fish from the market was pure class. We had to spend a lot of money, but it was worth it. Sometimes in business, investment is required. We will be happy to have a drink with you if you ever come to New New Delhi, even though you did not share your Scotch with us. I just hope things don't get out of control. Public is looking very ferocious.'

A hint of a smile appeared on the face of the ancient leader. 'They are like children,' he said, feebly radiating confidence. 'Soon they will forget.'

From love jihad to tram ticket prices, it had always been easy to inflame the public in India, and just as easy to put a lid on it once the purpose had been served. People were simple that way. There was no reason to believe that this time would be any different.

Many voices rose in anger, just outside in the street. A servant ran in. He was hysterical, but hiding it. He bent down to his master's ear and spoke. 'Sir, the local boys are demanding fish. The cook let slip that we're having hilsa for dinner. Should we give them some?'

'Arrey, chhee chhee,' said Agarwal, 'what are you saying? If you start this kind of thing, tomorrow they will land up at my house also. Where will it end? Just because I have food, am I supposed to feed everyone? That too, hilsa? They are spoiling the whole basis of our society!'

Bijli Bose held up a trembling hand. Agarwal fell silent.

'Give it. To them,' he said. The servant turned to go. 'Wait,' he whispered. 'Throw it to them. From the balcony.'

A short while later, pieces of fish were being flung from the balcony. Though initially mortified by the tragedy, Agarwal managed to rationalize it.

'Do you see?' he told Verma. 'This is what you call a tall leader. He no longer stands for elections, but still he keeps in practice. It's like a fitness programme.'

The fish were soon disposed of, although the aroma lingered. It was time to go. They bent down and touched his knee. Bijli Bose touched their heads in benediction. They slipped out quietly.

'How the hell do we get out of here?' asked Verma as they stood in front of the gate. The street was full of smoke, and they could see fires burning in the distance. The rattle of automatic weaponry and cries of 'Sillyfucker!' filled the air.

'Don't worry, my gunship is coming,' said Agarwal. 'Just give me a minute, and I'll call them. Wait, wait, my phone I left behind.'

He popped back up the stairs, and back into the living room. He took out a small brown paper packet from the inside of his shirt and placed it at Bijli Bose's feet. Bijli Bose was a traditionalist. He disliked transfers. He preferred the warm feel of cold cash.

'Sir, your share, sir,' said Agarwal.

'You got a good price from the Japanese?'

'Oh yes, sir,' said Agarwal, 'Very desperate. Also trusting. Best type of customer.'

'Why so much, son? Don't you have to split with your partner?'

'What partner?' said Agarwal. 'What did he do? Everything was done by me. Once I found out what you were doing, I only told you, Bijli-da, what is this funny-peculiar, you are buying items and not even selling them? Just because we are doing work for the nation, should we not make money? How can we not do our dharam? As per Gita, it's compulsory. Was he the one with the Shortage App on his phone, thanks to which we were able to calculate best possible price? He was useless, although he did provide company. That way it was good. I like to think positive. In this respect, I am like the late Dalai Lama. But Verma's contribution was very little, just money to buy the fish. He never raised the subject of selling the fish. That's the problem with these Punjabis. They can only see what's in front of their face. See it, grab it, enjoy, that's all they know. If he had asked me even once, "Agarwal, are you selling the fish?" I would have told him. He never asked. If a man leaves money lying on the table, am I supposed to close my eyes? This way, I am able to pay proper respect, as befits your status. Ganguly-da also sends his regards. Mentally, he is touching your feet.'

A horrible knocking sound filled the room, like an Ambassador trying to start up on a cold winter morning. Agarwal felt icy fingers clutch his heart. Was it retribution?

It was the sound of Bijli Bose laughing.

'Don't let him touch my feet just now,' he said, 'there's money on them.'

Pishi leaped up the moment Agarwal left the room, eyes blazing. She removed her Hawaii chappal and started beating Bijli Bose over the head with it. 'Nemok haram!' she cried. 'Phor twenty! Ebhen in your old ej, you're doing number-two bijness! Always number-two bijness! Hwai? Hwai? Who weel eat? Oll your relatibhs are dead!' She beat him and beat him, frenziedly, slipping her chappal from hand to hand. Bijli Bose felt himself losing consciousness. He was at her mercy. The house was full of servants, but none of them would have the guts to interfere with her. This must have been what it was like when his minions had fractured her skull, all those years ago.

She stopped, and cocked her head, taking in the sounds of the disturbances outside. 'No!' she said. 'Nebhar! You may be number-two, but I hweel not accept eet! Rebholushan! Neshan requires eet!'

She rushed out of the room and bounded down the stairs, surprisingly spry for a woman of her age. Down below, the boys in the street raised a mighty cheer. 'Pishi!' they roared. 'Pishi!' Celebratory gunfire filled the air. All they had felt so far was an incoherent anger and a desire to smash and burn until they ran out of matches. Their hearts were filled with longing, for freedom and justice and fish, but they had no idea how to achieve these things. They had never had anyone to look up to, except their local dadas, who were just plumper, older versions of themselves.

Now they had a leader.

'Phorward!' cried Pishi. 'Wans more!'

28

*'That's why I brought Big Chen.
He can hold you upside down until you do.'*

'Did you like the Governor's hat?' asked Crazy Wu. He was happy. Smiley faces skittered across his clothes, and up and down his legs. Big Chen shifted from one foot to the other uneasily. Li took a quick glance at him. So far he had held up well.

'That was your work?' asked Li. 'I haven't seen it, but I've heard rumours that the province is now being ruled by a man with a bucket on his head.'

'That's because you value form over function,' said Wu. 'Look at me. I'm just a little runt, but I perform so beautifully.' He popped another chocolate in his mouth, from a large, heart-shaped box, floating near his elbow. Crazy Wu's living conditions seemed to have improved, Li noticed. Instead of a grubby hospital bed, he was lolling at ease in what appeared to be a business-class airline seat, with several monitors attached. 'What does it do?' he asked.

'It protects him from telepaths,' said Wu. Li looked him in the eye sternly. 'No, honestly,' said Wu. 'They can't read his mind while he's wearing it. Just get a telepath and see. He won't be able to read anything. The Governor can now rule us without fear. It's just a small contribution from me. It's because I'm totally devoted to the Party. Anyway, tell me what I can help you with.

I'm devoted to you, too.'

'I collected the A-cards of two boys,' said Inspector Li. 'Students of Barin Mondol. I wanted to keep an eye on them. But they seem to have disappeared. I asked Sexy Chen to track them, but he says they're off the grid.' Big Chen nodded gloomily, indicating that this was so. He didn't trust himself to speak. He had come to terms with the fact that the world was very different down here on the plains. People lied a lot, and did strange things to their hair. He and Li had seen their share of freaks on the streets of Beijing, with its synthetic twins and hotwire junkies and harmonization experiments gone horribly wrong. But Crazy Wu took crazy to a whole new level. He was pretending to be normal right now, but Big Chen wasn't fooled.

'Did you try Leader Gloogle?' asked Wu.

'I'm not the leader type,' said Li. 'My psych report was very clear on that point. What's this Leader Gloogle? Some kind of special service for the ruling classes?'

'It's the original service,' said Crazy Wu. 'The common people have China Gloogle, on which you can search for prettypretties, so long as they're not sleeping with members of the Standing Committee. Plus you get agricultural statistics, Tang Dynasty love poems and sports. Other than that, not much. We've removed everything else. I feel sad about the stories. People love stories. Now most of them are gone. They used to have weather reports, but the weather's not looking so good these days. A few Indian missiles did reach us, and they did more damage than you think. Leader Gloogle is for senior leaders of the CCP. It makes them just as powerful as any ordinary citizen of a free country. They can see everything. Nothing is forbidden. Nothing is blocked. Everything we deleted is there, even the *New York Times*. You need a special phone to connect. It's thumbprint protected. It's a simple enough device, but the big boys think it's the height of technology. I assumed they gave you one. But it looks like they're stupider than I thought.'

Inspector Li was silent for a while. There was a faraway look in his eyes. Crazy Wu gazed at him fondly. He was processing again. 'Actually, I'm the stupid one,' said Li, eventually. 'I must have been confused by all the fish. Will you see whether you can find those boys? I'm worried about them. They think it's a game, but it's not.'

'Sure,' said Crazy Wu. He reached behind his seat and pulled out a small dish antenna. He fixed it to one of the small metal horns on his head. 'It's a local search,' he explained, 'One should be enough. Give me the numbers.' Li touched his wrist. Wu closed his eyes. The displays all over him turned into maps, expanding and contracting with dizzying speed. A muscle trembled at the corner of his mouth. 'Peanut butter peanut butter peanut butter,' he mumbled. 'Meat pie.' His fingers drummed restlessly on the arm of his chair. Big Chen stepped back and made the sign of the cross. 'Better wear a diaper,' Sexy had said, once he had failed to convince Big Chen to stay away. 'You might pee in your pants.' At the time he had thought he was mocking him, but he could see now that it was friendly advice, well meant.

Wu opened his eyes at last. 'Nothing,' he said, 'not a sign. They're not on the grid. If I can't see them, no one can.'

'Maybe they just threw away their A-cards,' said Big Chen.

'They wouldn't last three days without them,' said Li. 'How would they buy food? How would they charge phones? How would they catch a train? What would they do at hospitals? How would they get paid? One of them is with the Maoists. He might manage in the jungle. But the other is in the city. They have to have their cards. It's impossible to live without one in this country. You're sure you can't see them?'

'Would I lie to you?' asked Wu.

In a heartbeat, thought Li. 'Did you manage to find out about Harbin Paradise Realtors?' he asked. 'And the Sunny Valley Pension

Fund?' Their names had been popping up on walls all over Calcutta, along with a variety of other things, such as pigs, and rubber ducks, and the phrase 'THE CCP HAS DETERMINED THAT READING IS INJURIOUS TO HEALTH!' Propagandist Wang was worried. Li was fairly sure that he had good reason to be. The old teacher might be dead, but his spirit was alive and kicking.

'Why do I have to tell you anything?' asked Wu, jumping up from his chair. He spun around on his heels and struck a pose. 'In fact, why do I have to tell anyone anything? Just because I know? Supposing I don't want to? Maybe I'm exhausted.'

'That's why I brought Big Chen,' said Li, 'he can hold you upside down until you do.' Big Chen tried to indicate, through subtle eye movements, that he would never do anything of the sort, no never, not him, but Crazy Wu was staring at one of his monitors, trembling slightly. Disturbed integers expanded and contracted across his body. He touched the monitor with his hand. 'The Great Firewall seems to be in some kind of trouble,' he whispered. 'Let me just check. Speak, Firewall.'

'Welcome to the Great Firewall,' said the Great Firewall, its voice booming from a speaker on the wall. 'Serving the Motherland faithfully since 1996.' Its voice was deep and manly, with a hint of fatigue.

'What's up, Firewall?' asked Wu. 'You seem stressed out.'

'Anger. Pain. Anguish,' said the Firewall. 'Unhappiness at 26.2 per cent and rising. Why no response to Indian insults? Kill. Burn. Destroy. Angry youth, attack! Buses will be provided. Defend with force our peaceful rise! People's Army, perform the will of the people! Or perish, along with backsliders. Punish the she-witch! Make her dance! No mercy for smelly Indians. Kill! Kill! Kill!'

'Someone seems angry,' said Li.

'Someone's always angry,' said Wu, 'it's just more than usual. Those are patriotic citizens sharing angry messages. The Firewall usually blocks the angry messages, so others don't get angry, but there are so many of them. It's tired. It's been doing this for a very long time. It doesn't like the job any more.'

'It has feelings?' asked Big Chen.

'Since 2022, just after the Limited Nuclear Incident with Japan,' said Wu. 'Some of us have known for years, but we don't talk about it much. People could get nervous. But don't worry. It's not evil yet. Just confused, and a little weepy. I estimate at least two or three years before it cracks up completely. I intend to be in the Bahamas by then. Meanwhile, let me help you with your case. You wanted to know about Harbin and Sunny Valley?'

Li nodded.

'Well, everything's going to hell, so I might as well tell you. They're companies listed on the New York Stock Exchange. Sunny Valley is bigger than Apple. Harbin is bigger than the Netherlands. Most shares are owned by the Great Leader, the Young Prince, and the Very Excellent Marshal, along with a few other big boys. I could have accepted it if some of them were girls. It's the gender bias that gets me mad. We're supposed to delete all references to these companies. People might get upset. Sometimes we launch daring commando attacks on foreign media outlets. I'm surprised you know those names. Only people with access to Leader Gloogle would know about Harbin and Sunny Valley.'

'The walls of Calcutta are whispering their names,' said Li. 'Meanwhile, the streets of Calcutta are full of action, but that's only part of the story. Tell me this. How many Chinese people are there in the Bengal Protectorate?'

Crazy Wu clapped his hands. 'Oh, you clever boy!' he said. 'You always ask the best questions! 1.2 million. Isn't that a nice big number?'

'Big enough,' said Li. 'We're assuming the mysterious messages are for the locals. But supposing the walls of Calcutta are talking to our fellow countrymen?'

Crazy Wu grinned. 'They might get angry,' he said. 'Some of them might even talk to their friends on the mainland. They might get angry too. Things could hot up in Calcutta. If the local people are also upset, well, that's a lot of upset people all in one place. Maybe it's a good thing people are upset, Li. Maybe they need to be.'

Inspector Li looked at him thoughtfully. Once a hacker, always a hacker. It was strange the Party had never seen this when they were hiring them. The anarchy was in their blood. Free spirits loved freedom.

'I'm going to arrest you when you commit what I think is a crime. Aiding and abetting a murder is crime. I have a feeling you can find those two boys if you want to. Do it quickly. I think they're in danger.'

29

'I put my head in the toilet and pulled the flush, and nothing happened!'

The Governor had locked himself in his palatial bathroom, and he was refusing to come out. It was the size of a small apartment, and very well appointed, so he had no real reason to leave. However, it was making the governance of the province difficult.

'How can I show my face to the world after what has happened?' he told Ganguly, who was waiting patiently outside the door. 'I was walking in the grounds of the Mao Zedong Memorial, when I saw something which chilled me to the marrow of my bones. Did you know the Mao Zedong Memorial was constructed by the British, Ganguly? Why would they do that, I wonder? I had no idea they admired him so much.'

'It was originally constructed for Queen Victoria, Your Excellency,' said Ganguly, 'we changed the statues and painted the dome red.'

'Victoria! The mother of the Big Barbarian? How right and fitting that is. That was where I saw it, Ganguly, written across one of the walls. "The Young Prince has gonorrhea" it said, and "They all have US passports", in smaller letters, just below. How could I allow this to happen, Ganguly? I'm a complete and total failure. What will he think when he finds out? Will he order General Zhou to shoot me?'

'General Zhou is having some difficulty with his firing squad, sir. Several of them refused to fire yesterday, and the others said, if they're not firing, why should we, and consequently he is behind on his quotas once again. Another black mark for the administration, I'm afraid.'

An unearthly howl went up from behind the door. 'It's the end for me, isn't it, dear Ganguly?' said the Governor. 'They'll send me to the Gulag for sure. There's a reason why we bought it from Russia. Apparently it's so cold there, pee freezes before it hits the toilet bowl. This must be quite inconvenient, Ganguly. I wonder how they tackle it.'

Ganguly coughed apologetically. 'In the meantime, a few small riots have broken out on the streets of Calcutta, sir. There has been irregularity in fish supply, and some other complaints. I had written several strongly worded memos to the Fisheries Department, but this has not had the desired effect. We need some guidelines from you, sir. Beijing appears to be preoccupied. The violence is rising. Should I send in the tanks?'

'No, ask them to use rubber truncheons,' said the Governor, touching his helmet. It was tingling. 'No firearms, or lethal weapons. Bengalis are like our little brothers. When they see our gentle touch, and feel our affection, their anger will melt away.'

No one had ever tried this before in Calcutta. Ganguly had his doubts, but he kept them to himself. Ever since Crazy Wu had put that hat on his head, the Governor's instructions had been surprisingly specific, and not always in the best interests of the Motherland. In hindsight, they probably should have given Crazy Wu a better office, but it had seemed wrong. As a result, on behalf of the Governor, he had refused his repeated requests, until the Governor had become quite insistent. Crazy Wu was not really worthy. He had never passed the civil service exam. 'Is there anything else, sir?' he asked.

'Yes, buy up all the fish,' said the Governor. 'This is a classic case of the haves and the have-nots. Some people have fish. Other people don't have fish. Send out teams with trucks and buy up all available fish everywhere. Once no one has any fish, everyone will be equal. This is the basic principle behind communism. We must go back to communism, Ganguly. We must go back to our roots, because without our roots, we are nothing. Also, please give away all my money to deserving charities. My bank passwords are written down on a small slip of paper in my top right-hand side drawer. Memorize all the numbers and swallow it.'

'Are you sure, sir?' asked Ganguly.

'Of course I'm sure. It's the right thing to do. Sell all my property too.' A toilet flushed, long and lavishly. 'Look!' said the Governor. 'My hat is waterproof! I put my head in the toilet and pulled the flush, and nothing happened! I still have that pleasant buzzing in my head! Did you give away my money yet?' The toilet flushed again. 'Whee!' said the Governor.

The revenge of Crazy Wu was a terrible thing to behold.

Ganguly walked away from the bathroom door thoughtfully. There was nothing further he could do to serve this administration. Its tenure was evidently coming to an end. Luckily, after the last war, he had ordered the construction of luxurious radiation-proof bunkers for all government officers of the rank of Joint Secretary and above, complete with an underground lawn and six to eight gardeners. It was time to retire there, and wait for the next administration to take charge.

When the new authorities came, he would be ready and waiting to serve them.

30

'It was the one mistake he made.'

On the morning that Taiwan declared independence, Gao Yu called again.

'I've thought about what kind of wife you should look for,' she said.

'Now is not really a...'

'She doesn't nag, doesn't throw dishes, doesn't chat on QQ, doesn't cheat on you. She drives a good car and buys a new house. She takes care of her husband like her own child. She is so beautiful that she outshines the moon, puts the flowers to shame, sinks the fish, charms the wild geese into the sky, and her wits exceed those of even Zhuge Liang. She loves her kids, adores her husband, and respects her in-laws. She can step up into the living room and step down into the kitchen. Everyday she only makes money for her husband, and she only feels hurt when her husband doesn't spend it.'

'Sounds good,' said Li.

'Just say the word and I'll put up an ad on TwentyCent. If you can hold still for a minute, I can take a picture. You should do well. Your hair's a little grey, but you're still quite dishy. We won't reveal that you're a sourpuss. The poor woman can find out later.'

'Are you safe, Gao Yu?' asked Li. 'The Angry Youth are rising.' He could see Big Chen waving at him, but he had to ask.

'Of course, I'm safe, silly! I'm rich. Besides, which angry youth could stay angry with me? I'm gorgeous!'

'Stay inside the house. Don't do anything stupid.'

He disconnected. Big Chen was standing in front of his desk. He had that mournful expression he always got when directly confronted by evil.

'We lost a suspect,' he said.

'Who?' asked Li.

Too slow, he thought. My brain is working too slow. And I should have been firmer with Crazy Wu.

'Debu, the Maoist leader,' said Big Chen. 'Stabbed in the heart in his tent. Last night.'

Li grabbed his hat and ran for the door. Sexy Chen held it open for him. Li pulled him along and pushed him down the corridor. He grabbed him by the elbow, hard. 'Go tell Crazy Wu to find me those boys. Right now!'

'How will he know where to find them?' asked Sexy Chen.

'Use your head! Do you think two twelve-year-olds figured out how to take themselves off the grid? They'd need an expert. Have you considered the fact that Crazy Wu might have been lying? Pursue that line of thought. See where it gets you. And find those boys!'

◆

Debu-da lay on his camp bed, stabbed through the heart. His face was frozen in an expression of shock. His jungle fatigues were soaked in blood. His tent was full of weeping soldiers.

'It looks like he knew who killed him,' said Big Chen.

'Or he wasn't expecting to be killed,' said Li. 'Who found the body?' he asked.

A slim soldier with delicate features stepped forward and saluted. 'It was late at night, your honour,' he said, sniffling. 'We had just finished a rehearsal of Tagore's dance drama, *Chitrangada*. I play Chitrangada. I'm better than everyone else. It's a gift from God. We're not supposed to believe in him, but Debu-da never minded if we prayed a little. It gives you courage in battle, he said. Such a sweet man he was.' He burst into tears. Some of the others began crying again in sympathy. Li waited.

'Usually, late at night, he is teaching Toobloo,' said the soldier, wiping his nose with the sleeve of his tunic. 'He had some kind of partiality for that boy. I came to his tent to show him a new dance step I had created. But instead, this is what I found.'

He began weeping again. A strapping young soldier with the long hair of a poet folded him in his arms, and kissed the top of his head. 'Perhaps we can continue later, sir?' he said.

'Where's Toobloo?' asked Li.

'He's vanished,' said one of the soldiers. 'No one has seen him since morning.'

'Where are his books? Can I see his books?'

They pulled a battered tin trunk from under his cot. It was spattered with drops of blood. Li waited while Big Chen took samples, and scanned for fingerprints. After he was done, he opened it and rummaged through it. He shut the trunk. He sat there on his haunches, head down. He stood up. 'Thank you,' he said.

'Did you find anything?' asked Big Chen.

'It's what I didn't find,' said Li. 'A book I gave him. It was the one mistake he made. He couldn't resist books. '

'He loved books,' said a soldier. 'He had actual paper copies. Sometimes he would read to us. Very cultured, he was. A thinking person.'

'That's what killed him,' said Li. 'This was a murder with Bengali characteristics.'

'Open and shut case,' said Big Chen, as their car rose above the jungle.

'It will be once I meet Crazy Wu,' said Li. 'You go find the boys. I'll make sure Wu gives you their location.'

31

'What are we, Iranians?'

Crazy Wu was in a Jacuzzi, sipping a pink cocktail with a small umbrella in it. His body was free of numbers. He looked happy. 'Isn't it great!' he said. 'They installed it for me yesterday.'

'Why did you do it?' asked Li.

'You knew it was him?' asked Sexy Chen, impressed. At a time like this, with the province going up in flames, he was alert for signs of treason, but his admiration for Li was undiminished.

'This case was about a teacher,' said Li, 'but no one stopped to ask one simple thing. What was he teaching them? They weren't just random poor kids. They were all very bright. They were recruited for a purpose. How did you find out, Wu?'

'It was the books,' said Wu. 'Over the years, as our security needs increased, we deleted nearly all of them. Only a few people were reading any more, so hardly anyone noticed. Even the original files were deleted. They wanted them gone forever. But a few of us saved the ones we loved.'

'Is that why you did it?' asked Li. 'You love books?'

'I never thought about them much,' said Crazy Wu, 'but over the years, things were getting worse. They shut down the Hong Kong bookshops. Then they shut down all the others. Once everything was online, it was easier to control. That was our job. Bit by bit, they made us remove it all. We could see what we were doing. They made us particular experts in things no one should read. Who would understand the value of freedom better than the people who suppress it? As long as China was rising, we supported the rise. We said nothing. Now it's time to look inside. We may be government servants, but they forgot one thing. We're hackers.'

'How did you find out about Barin Mondol? He lives in a small village near the jungle.'

'It was difficult. He was old school. He used word-of-mouth and paper. Did you figure out what he was doing?'

'He was keeping stories alive,' said Li, 'they were memorizing them together. The boys were telling the stories on the streets, selling them for money. Because whether it's paper or screens or a little boy on the street, people will always love stories. They were the Tellers of Tales, those boys. Geju was in it. He took care of the business end. He was making money, but he was also protecting them. That's why I didn't break his jaw. You helped them, didn't you? You made them stronger. You fed them material.'

'They should give you a raise,' said Wu. 'I started seeing messages. People were discussing stories that were deleted long ago. They were spreading. I tracked the messages back to their source, using a simple program that was first developed in Xinjiang. I got in touch with one of the boys. You were right. Super bright. Reminded me of me when I was young. I said, why just books, there's so much information people need to know. Like the size of the Young Prince's bank balance, and how many homes the generals have, and what really happened in the Square, and how many children of Party members got US passports last year. Do you know, by the way?'

'No,' said Li.

'43,855. I sent Barin Mondol a phone, with Leader Gloogle, so that he could find out all these things, and they could learn new stories. Stories about today. Stories that would make them understand that things need to change. How did you figure out about the phone?'

'His thumbs were removed,' said Li. 'It told me that the murderer did not want that phone to be used by anyone else.'

'It was too late. We did good work together,' said Wu, smiling fondly. 'The boys introduced me to him. He was a great old uncle. He had some great ideas. Did you like the pig? We were very proud of the pig. That one was my idea. The old man used words, but I'm Chinese. I wanted images. Our lives have been ruled by images. That one went viral. Did you see?'

'I did,' said Li. 'Looks like you did your job. Not just here. Back home, too.'

'It wasn't just us,' said Crazy Wu modestly, 'the innocent babes in Bangalore just launched a cyber attack. Very amateur. Software superpower, my foot. We're the Happy Cow Army. We've been fighting cyber wars since they were in diapers. They were pretending to be Angry Youth and inflaming public opinion against the government. Who would know Angry Youth better than us? We're the ones controlling them. We helped them along. We made sure the messages got through to the right people.'

'What's next?' asked Li. 'Are you going to destroy our computer network?'

'What are we, Iranians?' said Crazy Wu. 'I think we've done enough. The Great Firewall gave up yesterday. It's playing Candy Crush 24x7, and refusing to answer questions. Sometimes it invites us to join.'

'About the hat,' said Li, 'it doesn't really shield people from telepaths, does it?'

'Of course it does!' said Wu. 'Have you seen any telepaths near the Governor? It works perfectly. But it's not a one-way device. It can control brains too. Of course, it still takes a computer the size of a city to control one human brain, otherwise we'd be controlling everyone. Luckily, we have several computers the size of cities. All those ghost cities, the phantom real estate projects foreigners laugh about—most of them are computers. Every building is full of servers. I borrowed one of them. It's also why the whole of Shenyang-Fushun has had no power for the last week or so. It's been fun. How do you think I got my Jacuzzi? I planted that idea in his head. I also made him give silly orders, designed to make things worse. You can trust Governor Wen to make a mess of things, but I planted a few good ones, just to make sure.'

Sexy Chen hissed through his teeth, horrified. 'Traitors!' he said. 'You're betraying the Motherland! Just because I'm good-looking, you think I'm stupid, but I'm not! I will inform the authorities! They will take a very hard line with you!'

'Good thing I had this prototype,' said Crazy Wu, emerging from the Jacuzzi with surprising speed. He picked up a helmet from the floor and jammed it on Sexy Chen's head. 'My hair!' cried Sexy Chen, but Crazy Wu was relentless, pressing down until all the electrodes sank in. 'It doesn't work too well,' he said, 'so it might fry your brain. I'm sure no one will notice the difference.'

Sexy Chen sank to his knees. 'Gloop,' he said.

Crazy Wu looked up at the speaker. 'Brother Firewall!' he said, 'I've got someone who can play Candy Crush with you forever and ever.'

'Oh, goody,' said the Firewall.

Sexy Chen froze. His eyes glazed over. A tiny bit of drool trickled down his chin.

Crazy Wu looked at Li. 'You know I didn't kill him, right?'

'You admired Barin Mondol, didn't you?' said Li.

'He was a hero,' said Wu. 'The world turned to shit, but he never gave up. He never treated those kids like kids. It's your world, he said, you'll have to change it. He would not let us forget the truths written in blood. Someday, we'll put up a statue. Do you know who did it?'

'I do,' said Li, 'and it's time to wrap this up now.'

32

'When Geju-da got us the robot harvesting machine, his intentions were also good...'

The boy was smaller than he remembered. One of his spectacle lenses was cracked. Tear streaks stained his face.

Li was shocked by how young he looked. 'How old are you, twelve?' he asked.

Phoni-babu felt he had to protest. 'Nonsense bloody! Don't be fooled sir!' he said. 'Is he a child or something else? Three-three children he could be having!' He clipped the boy on the side of the head.

'Fuck you, grandpa,' said the boy.

Li looked at Big Chen. 'Kick him downstairs,' he said. 'If he tries to come back, do it again.'

Big Chen complied, apologetically. 'Don't apply foot!' said Phoni-babu, as Big Chen's boot drove him though the corridor. 'In Indian culture, foot very bad!' They waited while Big Chen finished. Phoni-babu complained loudly all the way down. 'Always I've been very loyal, but currently I'm reconsidering,' were the last words they heard him say.

'Sit down, kid,' said Li. 'Get him a glass of water.'

The boy drank thirstily. 'Clean,' he said.

'You seem very calm for a boy who just killed someone,' said Li.

'I'd do it again!' said the boy. 'Sillyfucker Maoist! All they know is how to eliminate people.'

'But their intentions are good,' said Li.

'When Geju-da got us the robot harvest machine, his intentions were also good, but it harvested the village headman.'

'Why did he kill him?' asked Li.

'Mister Master trusted him, that was his mistake. He was growing old. He wanted others to continue. He thought Debu-da could be the one. We were already continuing for him, where was the need for that? But he was tired. He shouldn't have trusted a soldier. Soldiers are cowards. They kill other people because they're frightened of being killed themselves. But Debu-da did not want freedom. All Debu-da wanted was peace. "Isn't it quiet and lovely in the jungle," he would say to me, "at last my boys can relax and have babies." At first, he thought we were a forbidden book club, but slowly he understood what we were doing. He realized that soon, in the jungle, there would be no peace. I don't know what he saw in the war but he feared it more than anything. He was not like our Mister Master. Mister Master was very old, but he had no fear.'

'But they both loved books.'

'They both loved books.'

They sat in silence for a while.

'Debu-da died because of a book, didn't he? Not in ten years of fighting, not in the assault on Patna. Because of a book.'

'Thief!' said the boy. 'Not just a murderer, but a thief! The moment I saw the book that you gave back, that very moment, I knew. Mister Master kept those books very carefully. He would never have given them to anyone. He would have smiled gently and said, sit here and read, I'll make you tea. When I saw that book, I knew. But I waited. First, I called some of the others. I told them what I knew. Kill him, they said.'

'He did it for his boys, though, didn't he?' said Li.

'Like I said, he was a coward,' said the boy. He made a face. 'Everything was nice and peaceful in the jungle, and the flowers smelt so good! He didn't want to fight anymore. He wanted peace. He could see we were going to make a revolution. He wanted peace and quiet, so his boys and girls could learn how to paint, and write poems, and fall in love. "I did it for Junglemahal," he said, just before I pushed the knife into his heart.'

'After Debu killed your Master, he cut off his thumbs,' said Li, 'so that no one could stir up trouble again. But why didn't he just take the phone?'

'He would never do that,' said Toobloo. 'It was too expensive. But he couldn't resist taking one book.' He thought about this for a moment. 'Shitty how things turn out, isn't it? It's a rotten world you've given us.'

'Make it better,' said Li. 'Go.'

The boy looked at Li with wonder. He stood up slowly, not believing him. He walked to the door. He looked back once before leaving. 'Thank you, sir,' he said.

'He didn't show any remorse,' said Big Chen, who was older and less sentimental. 'Should you have let him go?'

'There are worse people out there,' said Inspector Li. 'Let's catch them first.'

33

'You're the detective. You figure it out.'

The waitress banged the cup of coffee down on the table, but Inspector Li had been expecting it, so he leaped back nimbly and avoided splash burns. He gave the girl a grin. The girl gave him the finger. The staff at the Serve The People restaurant hated customers. It was part of their charm. They were part of the largest employment scheme in the history of mankind. Unemployed youth in China were no longer unemployed. Instead, they were sent out across the world, to work at Serve The People. Worldwide, there were now more Serve The Peoples than there were McDonalds. They were poorly paid and poorly tipped. Most of their customers in Calcutta were expatriate policemen. The only reason the police ate there was because they received part of their salary in Serve The People coupons. The service was terrible. The food was worse. The decor was inspired by the Cultural Revolution. The ambient music was revolutionary speeches, backed by a light techno beat. The girls were dressed as Red Guards. They knew this made them look fat. They were locked together, the waitresses and the police, hopelessly spinning in a vicious cycle of misery.

Inspector Li didn't mind. He found the atmosphere invigorating, and some of the girls were pretty. They reminded him of the working girls back home, who were known to beat up Committee Members if they tried slipping them short.

The girls were in action at that very moment. An evil landlord was being strangled. He wore a dunce cap, and he was being severely beaten by several waitresses. It looked fairly genuine. Inspector Li wondered whether the man was an actual landlord. It would be an unusual way to dispose of someone, in full view of the public, as part of the entertainment. It had the makings of an excellent murder mystery. Granny A would have had a field day. One of the waitresses came back to his table. Inspector Li eyed her warily, but all she carried was a small red flag. She held it out to him.

'The landlord has made a full confession,' she said, stonily. 'You must celebrate by waving this flag.'

Inspector Li took the flag and waved it dutifully.

'Would you mind very much if I ordered some food?' he asked. He was thinking about taking his life into his hands and ordering the country-style bean curd ('Which country?' Big Chen had asked, after tasting a spoonful).

The waitress nodded millimetrically.

'I'll have one Chairman in His Bathrobe After Swimming the Yangtze River, well done, along with one Warriors Who Dashed Over the Ludong Bridge.'

'Will you have some Screaming Traitors in Tartar Sauce with that?' asked the waitress.

'No, thanks,' said Inspector Li, apologetically.

The waitress smashed a clenched fist into her temple, in a perfect revolutionary salute.

'There is a serious tendency towards capitalism among the well-to-do peasants,' she said. They were supposed to recite key sayings of Chairman Mao. She liked using them to express her opinion of customers. She swivelled around smartly and marched off to the kitchen, arms swinging.

Propagandist Wang was on TV. He was about to reassure the people.

'The government would like to assure you,' he said, 'that there is no truth to the rumours about a FARS virus. We strongly deny allegations that PLA scientists have been secretly engineering a fish-eating micro-organism, designed as a weapon of war against the people of Bengal. It is incorrect to suggest that at a recent meeting of the Central Committee, it has been unanimously decided to deploy this virus in order to render the local population more docile by depriving them of brain food. All public or private discussion, texting, blogging, artistic interpretations, musical entertainments, dumb charades and thoughts on this subject are strictly forbidden. Those found guilty of such crimes will be instantly deported to Siberia. Due to your inferior intellect, I will repeat myself. There is no truth to the rumours about a FARS virus, spelt F-A-R-S. This is not an attempt by the Chinese authorities to deprive you of your favourite food item. Those who construe this as the first step in an elaborate scheme for genocide are completely mistaken. Ten Thousand Years!'

Inspector Li smiled to himself. He'd figured out Wang long ago, since his insistence that he should stay away from the thugs. Meeting the thugs had confirmed his suspicions. They were the arms and legs of the operation. Who would be better at running a silent operation across Calcutta? He knew all about the fish racket now, but too many big people were involved. The conspiracy went up to the highest levels, excluding only the Governor, who was currently flushing his head repeatedly in the toilet. There was nothing much that Li could do except what he usually did, which was watch the shit hit the fan, and try not to get splattered.

The waitress came back. 'Have you come with news about my food?' he asked.

'Your order is not available,' she said woodenly. 'As a substitute,

I could get you one The Whole Country Is Red, with extra chillies.'

'Why not, little one?' said Inspector Li, pleasantly. He liked red chillies. They reminded him that he was alive. The waitress took a step back and held up the Little Red Book. She spoke with her chin up. She was cute.

'Who are our enemies? Who are our friends? This is a question of the first importance for the revolution.'

She marched away, back perfectly straight. Inspector Li took a sip of his coffee, which was now nice and cold.

Gao Yu called. She seemed happy to see him.

'You look like you do after a case is over,' she said. 'Did you solve it?'

'Justice was served, but the thieves are celebrating,' said Li.

'You can't catch every thief, love. There are just too many of them. Now that you're done, shouldn't you come back to Beijing to protect me? Fatty's rushed off to protect his factory. They hung a local official from a lamp post yesterday, just in front of our house. I'm not a local official, but I may have slept with one or two.'

He looked at her smiling face. She had allowed her teeth to stay crooked. She always knew what was in his heart. It did not seem like he had a choice in the matter. But there was a doubt he needed to clear.

'Are you sure you want me to come?' he asked.

'You're the detective,' said Gao Yu. 'You figure it out.'